The Necr
Lich Lord Wars book 3
Marc Van Pelt

DEDICATION

For my parents who has supported every dream.

Timeline of the World of Mundial

Year

1MA - First War of Destruction Yucaipan Kingdom and Village of the Shadow Hunters re-established on Elvish Continent

44MA - Battle North of Aguerius Forest

118MA Lich Lords attack the Vatan Province

119MA - *Forest Spirit*

123MA - *Lich-El, Escape through the Sacred Forest, The Necromancer*
Lich Lords begin invasion of Aguerius Province

129MA - *Time Mage*

983MA - Necromian Kingdom established

1012MA - The Forjad Consortium is formed

1024MA - Formation of the Yucaipan Republic

1850MA- *Mathen's Flight*

1854MA - Human/Elvish War Begins, fall of the Necromian Kingdom and Yucaipan Republic. Establishment of Port Cutter

1857MA- *The Merchant Ship Cree*

1904MA - *Frost Wyrm*

MA= Mortal Age

Italics= Published Works

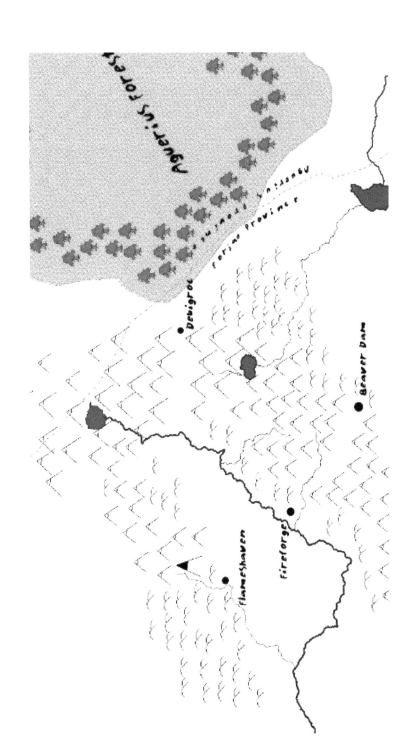

Chapter 1

"**Y**ou want to move all of our people to the Forjad Province?"

"Yes, we must strike before they have a chance to prepare themselves. We can't let the people here escape us like those in the Aguerius Province did."

"No matter how isolated the spot you have found for our camp, you are asking my Kadus Knights to bring their families to the front lines of a war zone. The extra guards we would need to post to protect them while we are away to battle–"

There will be no guards posted. We will need all our men for the battles. Aren't your people a warrior culture? Do you not train your young to defend themselves?"

"Lord Lich-El would never –"

"Lord Lich-El is still away, which means I'm still in command. You will do as you are ordered. Now let's hurry and bring your people here and set up our camp. We have a battle tonight."

THE LINE OF WAR WAGONS pulled by huge mammoths

proceeded towards the city that was protected inside a huge crack found inside an immense cliff face that stretched as far as one could see to the north and south. Inside the wagons, refugees from the Aguerius Province huddled together. In the basket of one of the lead mammoths, High Lord Gidon Aguerius looked over the caravan as it approached the city.

"Lord Mason!" A call rose up from the war wagon in front of the lumbering animal.

"Speak!" The lesser lord standing behind the high lord responded.

"Lady Izybel wishes to join you!"

Lord Mason stopped the caravan just long enough for Gidon's wife to exit the war wagon and climb up the rope ladder to the basket. As soon as she was in the basket, she spoke to Lord Mason.

"Stop the caravan outside the city wall. We will unload the refugees there."

"As you wish, your Ladyship. May I ask why? We can't be sure how far back the undead army is."

"Giddy told me he found a strange rock in our campground this morning. He said when we left the border of Aguerius Forest the stone became hot, and when he dropped it, the magic gate appeared right next to where it landed."

"A marked stone?" The elvish Lord Teanas asked, "In the Sacred Forest?"

"Someone in our group must have brought it with us! That is how they kept finding us!" Gidon exclaimed.

Izybel nodded, "We will need to do a complete search of everyone and everything we bring into the city."

"You think one of the refugees might be a Kadus Knight?"

Lord Mason asked.

"There could've been one among the people from any of the other towns. Not to mention 30 people my son rescued from an undead dungeon. There could've been a knight among them," Gidon answered.

"So, as I said, we search everything, and everyone entering the city," Izybel said.

"As you say," Gidon responded. All things aside, it was good to see his wife this way, in command. She was always so careful not to overstep her authority in the Aguerius Province, but now she was once more in her own lands where only her father had more authority, and she wore it well. It was one of the things that had attracted him to her. If he had to be in the predicament they were in, he was glad to be in it with this woman.

ALMAS WAS SITTING ON the ground looking at the walls of Debigroc as the soldiers conducted their search. He sat with Ulec, Cady, and Giddy who were talking to each other, but he wasn't paying attention.

His arm was hurting more by the moment and he was trying to push the pain to the back of his mind. He wondered how Ulec had been able to stand it for so many days.

When Ulec was dying of an infection from a cursed wound on his shoulder, Almas had somehow been able to not only see the curse but remove it to his own shoulder. They had been able to save Ulec but now the cursed wound was appearing on his own shoulder. Almas wondered how long before infection brought him down.

"Help me!"

Almas looked up, being pulled suddenly from his thoughts by the sound of his younger brother calling for help. He hadn't noticed Giddy wonder away from the group, and now Almas saw that he had gone over to one of the nearby mammoths. He must have grabbed hold of the animal's trunk and then failed to let go when the large beast raised its long nose up into the air. Now the young boy was hanging from the trunk high above the ground. Too high to drop comfortably, but not so high to put him in danger of being hurt.

Cady was the first to respond to the situation, "Serves you right. I told you to leave them alone."

"Ulec, tell him to let me down!"

Almas glanced at his elvish best friend. Ulec could speak to animals but by the mischievous expression on the young elf's face, he was likely the cause of Giddy's predicament.

Ulec called up, "He likes you. I think he wants to give you a nice big kiss."

"No!" Giddy cried as the mammoth began to lower the hanging boy down towards its mouth. Almas could see however that Giddy was laughing. The mammoth gave the boy a lick which made the boy laugh even more.

"Stop, that tickles," Giddy begged after receiving a second lick. After a third time the mammoth put the boy down, the hair on his head on the side he was licked standing straight up.

"That felt really gross," Giddy said, a huge smile betraying how he really felt.

The smile made Almas feel better, Giddy had been quiet and pensive the whole trip to the city. It was a marked stone that he had found that let Tornal create a magic gate to the refugees, which allowed the undead army to attack that morning and Giddy had nearly become the first victim of that attack. The close call had really scared the boy. It was good to see him returning to his normal self again.

Suddenly his thoughts were interrupted once again by a much older voice.

"Almas. Ulec. May I speak with you?

It was Lord Teanas. Almas stood, as did Ulec.

"Of course, Lord Teanas," Almas replied politely.

They walked off with the elf lord far enough from others that none would hear them.

Finally, Lord Teanas spoke, "Almas, tell me, what do you think of these city walls?"

A little surprised by the question Almas hesitated a moment before answering, "They...um...look strong."

"Yes, they are, try looking deeper."

So Ulec must have mentioned his newfound ability to see, or more accurately sense magic. Well that really didn't matter, he trusted Ulec's father. He tried to look deeper and after a moment he saw what Lord Teanas wanted him to see.

"The walls are infused with magic," Almas said in awe.

"Yes, they are enchanted, Lich-El himself couldn't even break up these walls. Now look at your crest."

Almas pulled his crest out from under his shirt and studied it. It also was enchanted and every few seconds a small pulse of magic shot out from it. Following the pulse of magic with his eyes he saw it went right to his father who was standing a bit away overseeing the search.

Other pulses were converging on his father and he realized

they were coming from his siblings and mother.

"There is some kind of connection to my father," Almas stated with a questioning voice.

"Yes, your father has your crest magically connected to a compass so he can find you in an emergency. It was how we found where you were so quickly. Such an item like the stone your brother found would behave the same way. That is what you need to keep an eye out for. Those pulses of magic going out towards the undead army."

Almas scanned around him but seeing the world through magical eyes was still so confusing. Turning back to Lord Teanas he started, "I'll keep an eye...out."

He hesitated part way through his response because he noticed for the first time Lord Teanas held enchanted items.

"Your ring is enchanted?"

Lord Teanas glanced down at the ring on his hand. "Yes, this ring is a fieles—Mimic."

"Mimic?"

Ulec answered for his father, "It has the power to change form to any weapon it has had contact with before. If it has come in contact with a fieles then it can also mimic the powers of that fieles when it takes its form."

With a flash of light, a sword appeared in Lord Teanas' hand.

"Wow," Almas exclaimed and then asked, "What about the thing in your pocket?"

Lord Teanas smiled as the sword vanished and answered, "That is why I want both you and Ulec. I have a gift for each of you."

The elvish lord brought out what looked like two bundles

of beads and strips of leather.

"This is called a rusica," He said spreading out one of the bundles.

It was a web of leather threads with colored wooden beads making a design that looked like a wolf's face with a brown background.

On one side if it, the leather strings were connected to a bracelet, while on the opposite side had four strings attached to four rings.

Lord Teanas slipped the bracelet around Almas' wrist and then slid the four rings on his fingers leaving out the thumb. The result was, the web covered the back of his hand.

The elvish lord then put the other one on Ulec's hand which had a design of a tree rather than a wolf on it.

"They are both enchanted," Almas stated.

"Yes, they are both connected. If you press the center bead with the intention to make the magic active–"

Lord Teanas pressed the center bead and Almas saw a small burst of magic shoot out to Ulec's rusica and a bead on it started glowing.

"–it will cause the other one to point and lead the one wearing it to you."

"So Ulec can find me if I want him to and the other way around?"

"Precisely, as both of you seem to have a habit of getting into trouble, I thought having a way to call and find each other would be prudent."

Lord Teanas handed Ulec his rusica who wordlessly studied it a moment before putting it on, then the elvish lord motioned for the two boys to follow him.

"Now I believe it is about time for us to enter the city, let us go."

The city was amazing, it was so different than other cities that Almas had seen of the Forjad Province during trips to visit his grandfather. After passing through the wall's gate, he came to a large plaza lined on either side by stables and barracks with sheer cliffs rising high above on either side. In the center of it was a huge boulder the size of a large building.

Beyond the boulder, the plaza ended with a wall of buildings with only a single road passing though the center into the city beyond. The road only went a few hundred feet before splitting into two roads that angled towards either side of the passage through the mountain, the city filling up what amounted to a crack through the cliff just wide enough for two or three city blocks.

It was the architecture of the buildings more than anything that made the city so different. Most were so much more rounded and curvier than ones found in other cities in the province. Almas realized these were original elvish buildings.

"What's in those jars?"

Ulec's sudden question brought Almas back from all the sights of Debigroc. Ulec was looking at a stack of jars next to a ballista on top of a barrack.

"The jars?" Almas asked somewhat surprised, "Those are Forjad Firebombs. The same things that the mammoth riders were using against the undead army this morning."

"What is it made from?"

"I don't know, it is a closely guarded secret. I figured you would have found it out a long time ago."

Ulec shook his head and said," This city is too far from

Aguerius Forest for me to easily see it."

They were silent the rest of the way. Most of the refugees were being sheltered in the city offices while the Aguerius family were given rooms in Lord Mason's home along with Ulec and his father.

The grownups went directly to war councils while servants saw to feeding the children and showing them to their rooms. Exhaustion from days of fleeing the lich lords' armies caught up to them, and they were all asleep before sun had even set.

Chapter 2

"**O**ur spy should be opening the gates soon. We must be ready to attack."

"I want to know why I won't be with my men."

"Lich-El was clear when he left that you were to take charge of our spy when he returns to us."

"Do you really think he will open the gates? We are betting a lot on him succeeding."

"He has no choice and no one will ever suspcct him."

TEANAS WALKED ALONG the side of the immense boulder in the courtyard between the city and the city gates with Lord Aguerius. Night had fallen and they walked in the shadow of the huge rock. They walked unseen by the sentries on the wall.

When they reached a depression in the side of the boulder Teanas put his hand on the side of the rock face and spoke an elvish word. An opening appeared in what a moment before had been flawless stone, revealing a staircase leading under the boulder.

As they began to descend the stairs Gidon commented as

much as asked, "And I suppose no one in this city is aware of this little secret passage?"

Teanas smiled as he responded, "No one ever asked for a list of secret passages or chambers when I gave up this land, but I'm sure they will find it someday. Humans always seem to start tunneling underneath their cities eventually."

Before Gidon could give any response, the stairs ended at the entrance to a large room with floor to ceiling shelves on each wall. The shelves were filled with books and manuscripts covered with elvish characters. There were also rows of bookshelves throughout the room.

"Nice library; now, why are we here?" Gidon asked after taking a long look around the room.

"I needed to look something up", Lord Teanas responded and then asked, "Almas still remembers nothing about how he was healed of his wounds?"

"No, he only remembers waking up in a room with Lich-El."

Teanas began looking through old tomes and manuscripts as he continued, "The hole in his shirt from the blast of magic was over his chest and his crest was badly melted. How serious would you say his injuries should have been?"

"They should have been fatal. The heat needed to damage his crest as it was should have burned deep into his chest."

"Could you have healed him if you had been present?"

Gidon hesitated a moment before answering, "No, my magic can only speed up natural healing, his lungs and heart should have been damaged beyond the ability to heal."

"So to heal him the lich lords would have had to create new flesh?" Teanas asked as he found several old bound pages and removed them from a shelf and sat down at a table with them.

Gidon answered, "Correct."

Teanas continued, "To my knowledge, all healing magic used by mortals follow the same principle. They can't heal what the body itself couldn't do if given the time. But unless the lich lords have an immortal Kaynarian God that didn't die in the War of Destruction, they found a way to do it."

"Let me guess, the book you found tells how to do such a thing?"

Teanas smiled and responded, "This contains a desert elf's research. It speaks of what he calls Creation Magic. The magic to change something's nature. While mortals are limited to using magic to manipulate the world around them. The gods could create new things. That is how they made this world and the life on it."

"Wait," Gidon put one hand up to interrupt Teanas as he clutched the bow hanging on his shoulder.

Teanas realized he was speaking with the fieles known as Sacred Knight. Suddenly Gidon continued, "If that is a power that only gods can use then how did my ancestor Lord Morin do what he did?"

"*Read the last page,*" came a voice to his own head. It was his own fieles, Mimic. The one in his ring.

Teanas turned to the last page and begin reading. After a few moments he found what he was looking for.

"It says here that Creation Magic requires huge amounts of magic. Mortals simply don't have access to the magic pools needed. Even in the rain forests where there are the greatest stores of Natela magic, there wouldn't be enough magic to do such a thing. A human would exhaust themselves before creating enough Trabar Magic. Lord Morin had Snipies' blood; that must have given him enough power to do what he did."

"So, you think they used Kaynarian blood to heal my son?"

"Let me speak to him," Mimic spoke out.

Teanas extended his right hand to Gidon, "Take my hand, Mimic wishes to speak to us."

The human did as they were instructed and listened.

"You are missing some important points. While what that snot-nosed lunatic of an ancestor of yours created was impressive, the important point is what he did to himself. He healed his mind and gave himself magic abilities.

"Now another human has been subject to the same kind of magic and what are the odds that after having been healed by this power that your seemingly generous enemies stopped there?

"Do you really think that after being under the influence of this magic, it's a coincidence that he suddenly developed a new magic ability? How they got the magic to do what they did is irrelevant. What is important is this; what other alterations did they make in your son?"

Gidon let go and stumbled back in surprise.

"No, that can't be," he stammered.

Teanas' mind was also racing. Tornal had wanted Seacra for some sort of experiment. Almas had taken the blast meant for her. It was very possible that he had become the subject of Tornal's experiment in her place as well.

"Lord Gidon, I hope Mimic is wrong but we need Almas to be watched at all times till we know for sure."

Teanas returned the pages to the shelf and was about to suggest they go find Almas when the muffled sound of horns started sounding from somewhere outside the rock.

"Are those...?" Teanas started to ask but was cut off by Gidon's answer.

"It's a call to arms...the city is under attack!"

ALMAS WAS HAVING THE nightmare again. The same one he had every time he fell asleep; the one he could never remember when he woke up.

He was back in Demon Mountain; in the same room he had woken up in right before he had met Lich-El. There was however something different, Lord Teanas was standing next to him.

"What are you doing here?" Almas asked.

Lord Teanas without looking at him answered, "I'm not. This is, after all, a dream. Perhaps we should see how it plays out."

Almas wasn't sure what he meant, but when he followed the gaze of the dream Teanas, he saw Lich-El and Tornal standing above a bed in which he saw himself lying in, asleep with his arms and legs bound.

The two Lich Lords were talking to each other.

"I gave one order and you couldn't even do that right?" Lich-El said angrily.

"I was able to save him!" Tornal defended.

Lich-El shook his head and accused, "He wasn't supposed to be injured to begin with, Tornal!"

"How was I supposed to know he'd jump into my attack?"

"The boy is an Aguerius; self-sacrificing for others is bred into the Paladin line. Why do you think after over a hundred years, Gidon and his children are all that's left of the line?" Lich-El explained.

"I think you're forgetting about your 'pet,'" Tornal countered.

"He abandoned that line years ago and the line has abandoned him. But he isn't what we're discussing. I'll be taking the boy into my personal custody from this point. I expect that is fine with you?"

"Yes...yes Lord Lich-El," Tornal agreed subdued.

"Is your experiment complete?" Lich-El asked.

"It is my lord, but I wish you had let me use the remaining prisoners; I would have liked to have altered his mind better, I think I could've bound his will more," Tornal complained.

"I have my own purpose for the remaining prisoners," Lich-El responded. "Now wake him."

Almas watched Tornal command his sleeping form to wake. He saw his own eyes open with a start and look around with an expression of terror.

"Where am I? What happened?"

"You were fatally injured defending your friends. Tornal was forced to conduct his experiment on you in order to revive you."

Dream Almas looked at the two lich lords standing above him in horror, "What did you do to me?"

Tornal answered, "I trapped you in the doorway between life and death. I altered you and have given you the ability to lean either way; lean out towards life and you are in your human form as you are now, lean out towards death and you can take the form of a lich lord with all the powers of one of us. Remember however, no matter how far you lean towards one you will always have one foot in the other so that you will never be completely human or undead."

Lich-El continued, "Tornal made a few other adjustments. You have the ability to see magic and steal magical traits you may find in others. Also, Tornal has enslaved your mind in that you must obey his commands."

"So that is what happened," Dream Teanas muttered.

Almas was too horrified to pay attention. This was simply a nightmare, it had to be. He would have remembered this.

Lich-El continued, "Now take your lich form."

Dream Almas continued to just stare in shocked silence and after a moment Lich-El turned his head to give Tornal a stern glare.

Tornal quickly said, "I order you to obey Lord Lich-El's command."

When Lich-El continued to glare expectantly Tornal quickly added, "All of his commands!"

Dream Almas suddenly gasped as his skin started to turn pale and his eyes turned a yellowish color. Spikes of bone began growing up and down his arms. In just a moment Dream Almas had transformed into a lich lord.

"Very good," Lich-El said, "this will be most helpful. Tornal, give me one of your marked stones, then you will leave us."

"But my lord, he is my experiment -"

"And I told you he is now in my custody! Leave us!"

Tornal backed out of the room cowering all the way out. Once he was gone Lich-El turned his attention back to Dream Almas.

"Time is short, your father is on his way here to rescue you. Here are your orders. I will soon order you back to sleep, you will wake up after two minutes and remember nothing of what you have seen and heard since we woke you up. After you are rescued, you will be trapped by a force of undead before you reach Jaspen. Make sure you are forced to flee west across Aguerius Forest to Debigroc in the Forjad Province. On the far western side of the forest, you will drop Tornal's marked stone. Then after you have reached Debigroc you will remember everything in a dream your first night there. You will then unlock the city gates and rejoin my army. You will obey all orders of the leader of the Kadus Knights from then on. Now sleep and forget."

Almas snapped awake with the sound of Dream Teanas swearing in elvish ringing in his ears. It took him only a moment to realize for the first time in weeks he remembered his dream...it was a dream, it had to be!

Almas closed his eyes to try to will himself back to sleep only to realize his eyes were still open and he was getting out of bed! He had to go open the gates to the city.

He shook his head; he couldn't do that! Yet there he was creeping out the door! Realization hit him that it hadn't been a dream, they had done something to him! He was the traitor! He had brought the marked stone that had allowed the undead to follow them to the Forjad Province. He remembered now that the stone had been in his pocket all that time; *he* had dropped it in the place where Giddy had found it.

He quietly left the building and began to make his way towards the city gates. He needed to figure out how he was going to open the gates. Wait, no! He needed to find a way to stop himself, lives depended on it; his family's and his friend's lives depended on it!

Almas made it to the courtyard between the city and the city gates. He couldn't pass without being seen so he didn't even try.

"What are you doing out at this hour?" The sentry immediately asked.

Almas tried to warn the sentry to stop him but instead found himself saying, "I need to find my father."

He lifted his crest into the light to make sure it caught the light of a nearby torch.

"Oh. Your father passed by here a little while ago with the elf. I last saw them near Sentry Rock," the sentry said indicating the huge boulder in the center of the courtyard.

"Thank you," Almas said as he left the sentry and entered the courtyard. Being the grandson of the high lord of the province had its privilege.

He moved around Sentry Rock and from its shadow looked around. There was no sign of his father or Lord Teanas. The barracks and stables were quiet. Only the sentries on the wall and by the gate were visible. The gate doors were thick metal with a large metal bar keeping them safely closed. Breaking it down was out of the question.

Almas looked closely at the flows of magic around the courtyard. He could see the Natela magic coming off of the men and also from the animals in the stables. Looking near the barracks he saw a different kind of magic.

It was emanating from a refuse pile on the side of the building. Rotting leftover food; fruit, vegetables, meat, and bones. As it decayed it slowly released a dark kind of magic.

An idea hit him, a terrible idea. He tried to banish it immediately from his mind but he was already moving towards the rubbish pile.

As he approached, he heard a familiar voice behind him. "Almas?"

It was Ulec's voice. He stopped in his tracks. His orders from Lich-El were to save Ulec's life; he couldn't kill him if he tried to interfere. The moment of relief that thought brought was quickly replaced once again by horror. What if someone else tries to stop him? What if someone from his family tried? He had to get away from those he cared for!

First, he needed to figure out how to both get the gates opened and not kill Ulec when his friend tried to stop him.

"Almas, what's wrong? You activated your rusica."

Almas glanced at the bracelet, rings, and beads on his hand. Sure, enough there were small bursts of magic leaving it and going to Ulec's rusica behind him. When had that happened? He didn't remember even thinking about activating it and calling for Ulec. In fact, the curse controlling him should have stopped him. What was going on?

Ulec gave him no time to consider it as he continued, "There are a few undead outside the walls just out of view of the sentries. We need to warn the guards!"

Time to plan was over, it was time to act. He felt that weird dark feeling that had been with him since Demon Mountain increase as his body took its undead form. He still had his back to Ulec and his cloak blocked him from seeing his transformation.

"They aren't just outside the wall. They are already inside." Was that a warning? Did he manage to act outside his orders? No, it was a distraction. Ulec's attention would be looking for threats nearby now, not on him.

THE NECROMANCER

Almas reached into his sleeve and broke off one of the bone spikes that had appeared up his arms when he had changed to his undead form. He threw the bone into the refuse pile and in a flash of darkness a horror appeared in the form of a mass of bones resembling the skeleton of a cow with long horns.

"Almas?" Ulec cried in alarm as Almas finally turned to face his friend. Ulec looked at him with a look of pure shock and terror.

Almas stared back with an undead face still stained with tears that had been falling freely a moment ago.

"Please stop me—kill me," he managed to say right before several fluttering masses of bones, resembling the skeletons of birds, jumped out from behind the larger bovine skeleton and pounced on Ulec.

The elvish boy immediately began thrashing about trying to throw off the pecking and scratching undead creatures. Meanwhile the bovine creature began charging at the city gate. It had made it more than half way before a horn sounded an alarm.

It was too late, the only guard that was able to try to meet the charging monstrosity was knocked to the side a moment before it hit the large doors which didn't even budge. As the other guard by the gate approached to attack, the skeletal cow lifted its head and used its horns to lift the large metal bar that was locking the doors. With a turn of its head it slammed the bar into the second guard.

Now many horns were sounding along the wall. The city was beginning to respond.

"Almas! What are you doing?"

Ulec had pulled his dagger out and Metal was out of its

bag spraying down one of the undead birds with acid. Ulec was cutting down the remaining creatures.

"I'm sorry! They did something to me, I can't resist their orders," Almas sobbed.

The city gates burst open as revenants and Kadus knights burst into the plaza. Outside the doors a magic gate could be seen glowing and pouring out an army. He had one more order, he ran to meet the invading army he had just unleashed on his family, friends, and thousands of innocent people.

Chapter 3

"Where did Tornal go?"

"He is by the magic gate. He must be near it to anchor this side of it in place. He is bringing in the remainder of our forces. They are already putting up a stiff resistance."

"He should be helping to secure the gate to the city. If we allow them to form an organized defense, we risk losing a lot of forces in winning this battle."

"Let us worry about taking the city. Just make sure your knights follow our orders, and see to your new charge. Here comes the boy now, he looks rather unhappy."

"He was just forced to betray his family, friends, and people. I'm sure he is not."

GIDON EXITED THE ROCK and stepped into utter chaos. The gates were open and completely overrun. The plaza was filling with combat as more attackers and defenders poured into it.

He was loading an arrow into his bow when a ballista on the roof launched a projectile at the city gates which erupted in an explosion of flames.

Gidon charged the arrow with magic and released it at a group of invaders! The arrow became a beam of light and all in its path disappeared! More explosions could be heard near the wall and Lord Mason's voice yelling above the noise of combat calling for a retreat.

The flames near the wall suddenly began spinning into several vortexes that suddenly began gathering into one huge flaming vortex in front of the gates, blocking more invaders from entering the plaza.

"Fall back from the walls!" Lord Mason's voice continued to call and Gidon caught sight of him on the front line of the fighting. He was cutting down any undead or knight that was preventing his men from retreating.

Lord Teanas walked past; his hands outstretched in front of him towards the flaming vortex. Fireballs began to shoot out of the vortex, each striking down a revenant or Kadus Knight freeing up more city guards to retreat as ordered.

"They've destroyed the doors; we have no way to seal the gates!"

Lord Mason came up beside Gidon and helped him cut down several more undead as he spoke.

"We will make a line of defense at the entrance to the streets and hold them there as we evacuate the city through the rear gates."

"Will you have time to prepare? Lord Teanas can't keep that up for long."

"He won't have too. We just needed enough time to get all my men off the wall," Lord Mason responded.

He then gave a hand signal in the direction of the barracks

and shouted, "Flame up!"

A line of stone pillars rose quickly from the ground to about 9 feet tall. They began spinning and belching out fire, creating a wall of flames.

"That should give us time to get my men into position," Lord Mason said as he and Gidon began jogging back towards the entrance to the city streets.

"What happened?" Gidon asked.

"I'm not sure, I haven't received a report from the men on the wall yet."

The plaza was a bustle of activity. Mammoths were being moved from the stables into the city streets, ballistae were being set up on the rooftops. Soldiers were everywhere with more appearing every moment.

"What can my men and I do?" Gidon asked.

"You can help the evacuation and guard my people till they get to Flameshaven."

"We should assist you and then cover your retreat. You should stay with your people."

"I appreciate your offer but as a strategist you know my men are best suited to defending this city and yours for seeing to their safety on the road," Lord Mason said flatly and before Gidon could respond, he called out to one of his guards, "Hartman!"

The guard stepped over to his lord and saluted.

"What happened to the gates?"

The soldier hesitated and gave a fearful look in Gidon's direction. Finally, he looked back to Lord Mason and said, "I heard a disturbance in the plaza. I saw two boys near the barracks, one seemed to be struggling with several small creatures while the other one watched. There was also some sort of beast made of bones running to the gates. I heard Guardsmen Cooper call out that there were undead outside the gates and so I called the alarm. The beast charged through the guards at the gates and used its horns to open them. Undead began to pour in from outside.

"Did you see who the boys were," Gidon asked, turning pale as a sickening feeling began to overcome him.

Again, the guard hesitated before answering, "It was dark but they appeared to be your second oldest son and his elvish friend."

Gidon felt his legs begin to become unsteady. Out of nowhere Lord Teanas was at his side steadying him.

"What happened to them?" The elvish lord asked.

Addressing Lord Teanas the guard answered, "Lord Aguerius' son left through the gates unopposed by the undead. I lost sight of the other."

If Lord Teanas hadn't been supporting him, he would have collapsed. They had his son...they had done something to HIS son.

Lord Mason grabbed and shook his shoulder, "Lord Aguerius! We have no time to deal with this now. They didn't harm him as he left, so right now your other children and wife are in more danger than he is. We have to get the people out of here!"

Lord Teanas added, "Wherever Almas is you can be sure Ulec will be near."

They were right. He had to somehow push everything to the side and focus on his job, he rescued Almas once and he would find a way to do so again but right now he had a job to do. He gave a shaky nod and found his own footing again.

"Hartman, take Lord Aguerius and Lord Teanas to oversee the evacuation."

Lord Teanas interposed, "If it is alright, I'd like to stay here and help for a while."

"Very well," Lord Mason said before turning and walking away.

"This way my lord," the guard said as he led Gidon away.

TEANAS WATCHED LORD Gidon walk away, his heart aching for the man. Lich-El had tricked them, they had done something to Almas and had given the boy back only to use him against them.

He was also plagued with worry about his own son. He was sure he had gone after Almas and while he had faith in his son's abilities, he hoped Ulec wouldn't underestimate Lich-El or Tornal.

Lord Mason was lining up his soldiers across the entrance to the city proper. They all had long tower shields with notches in the upper right-hand corner. The edges also had some strange grooves on them.

Once all the men were standing in ranks Lord Mason began speaking as he paced in front of his men.

"Look ahead of you!" The men looked; flames could be seen dancing in the sky high above and beyond the boulder.

"Death is before you; behind you is everyone you hold dear! You are the wall that separates them! Look at the men standing around you. If they fall, or you do, the wall will be broken and your loved ones might pay the price of our failure."

Lord Mason stopped pacing and facing his men ordered, "Lock shields!"

The first row of men stepped forward and attached their shields into a small grove in the cobblestone running along the width of the road. Once the first row was down the second line of men attached their shields on top of them. Several men then removed some cobblestones a few feet from the new wall of shields revealing holes from which they pulled out long beams of wood. They angled the beams down towards the wall and attached them. In a matter of moments, they had a ten-foot-tall wall reinforced with beams of wood.

The notches he realized provided small holes in the wall for archers to shoot arrows through or to push spears out.

Lastly several benches were brought out and attached to the bottom of the wall creating a rampart allowing the defenders to be able to attack the invaders from above.

"Lord Teanas, would you care?" Lord Mason asked as he gestured to one of the benches.

The elvish lord stepped up onto the bench and looked over the top of the wall. The glow of the flames had dimmed.

"Won't be long," Lord Mason said looking over the wall next to him.

"Would you have a quiver of arrows to spare?" Teanas asked.

"Would you like a bow to go with them?" Lord Mason asked raising a questioning eyebrow.

Teanas extended his arm and a bow flashed into existence. "Just the arrows will be fine."

"That is a nice trick," the human lord commented. A

gesture to his men and a quiver full of arrows was handed up to the elf.

The glow from the fires faded completely and shortly the sound of many feet on cobblestone could be heard. Then they appeared, marching rank after rank around either side of the boulder and then right towards the wall of shields.

"Ballista take aim!" Lord Mason called out. "Ready...Shoot!"

Small bottles shot out from along the roofs on either side of the defenders guarding the wall. Each struck among the ranks of undead and exploded into flames. Next it was the archers turn. At Lord Masons command, the archers open fired. Arrows poured out from the rooftops, from over the walls, and from the archer slits.

Lord Teanas fired arrow after arrow into the oncoming hordes with perfect aim. Line after line fell from the onslaught of projectiles. Then the first undead reached the wall. Spear points rushed from archer slits while arrows, stones, and exploding pots rained from above. Now those manning the top of the wall had to duck between shots staying clear from enemy arrows and bone spikes thrown from the revenants. As Teanas crouched behind the wall loading another arrow, Lord Mason asked, "Is it me or weren't they fighting much better this morning?"

Teanas stood and shot his arrow as Lord Mason threw an exploding pot before Teanas answered," They do seem more sluggish than normal. Perhaps we are facing a different Lich Lord controlling them."

"Whatever the case, it will still be a long night I fear."

ALMAS SAT WATCHING helplessly as more undead entered the city. His own body had betrayed him. He had left unopposed by the undead hordes to find Deleta outside the city with a lich lord. The Kadus Knight ordered him to sit down and returned to overseeing the battle with the lich, pointedly ignoring him.

He couldn't see the battle past the walls but he did see the whirlwind of fire blocking the gates. The sight kindled some feeling of hope. If anyone could save the city from being destroyed it was Lord Teanas. But the elvish lord could only block the entrance for so long. Soon the way would be opened again and everyone in the city would be killed.

He had to obey orders. Right now, the only one present that he had no choice but to obey was the leader of the Kadus Knights—Deleta. The only order he had to follow right now was to sit. So as long as he sat, he could do other actions he assumed, but what could he do? He didn't have any instruments, so no bardic skills. All he had was the necromancy abilities Tornal had given him. The thought of using that turned his stomach but what else did he have; everyone he cared about were in danger because of him, he had to try to do something.

There were a couple of problems however, the first being that there were no animal remains nearby to animate, the other being that using death magic for a lich was the same as an elf using Natela Magic; that when one used magic, others nearby could feel the drain the use of magic caused. He certainly could feel the Lich Lord using up a lot of death magic; so as soon as he tried using it the undead creature would know it. He needed to plan this out carefully.

The flaming whirlwind was starting to die down when Almas finally settled on a plan. First, he hoped that his necromancy skills applied to all dead remains, not just animal. He took his undead form and broke off one of the bone spikes on his arm. He then poked the spike into a stick lying on the ground. In a flash of darkness, the spike and stick disappeared and in their place was a long flute with its own bone-like spikes coming out the side.

"Hey!"

The Lich Lord had turned abruptly to face Almas. "That magic is mine. Your only orders are to sit."

"Sorry," Almas said cowering a little. "I just needed to make a flute so I could help you with the battle."

Luckily Deleta seemed to be ignoring him and he had no orders to obey the lich who now was looking at Almas with a somewhat confused look and seemed to be about to ask a question when Almas quickly put the flute to his lips and started playing.

If he directly used magic to work against the undead, then they would see it, resist it, and stop him. So, he had decided to try a more subtle approach. He started sending feelings of strength and power to those who could hear; making sure it was only the feeling and not the real thing.

The Lich's question was cut off before he had a chance to begin it. After a moment of being mesmerized by the music he spoke, "Lich-El was correct about you being an asset to us, just do not use my Mortai magic," and then he turned his attention back to the battle.

"I don't care what he can do. I should be fighting with my knights, not babysitting," Deleta growled not even glancing back to Almas.

"Had you led your forces into the city you would now be nothing but ash and smoke. Your babysitting task saved your life," the Lich Lord responded. Deleta didn't answer.

With no one watching him Almas continued to hold and play his flute with one hand while he used his other hand to remove another bone spike and stuck it into the ground in front of him. This was the moment of truth, did his magical abilities only work with certain kinds of magic or could he use different sources?

The ground he had put his bone spike in was full of dead leaves, twigs, dead insects and other formally living things too small to see. Almas tried using some of the magic he was creating with his flute, and in a small flash, his bone spike disappeared and a strange looking form appeared in its place.

It was a hand sized creature that looked to be made of assorted leaves and twigs. Like every undead thing Almas had ever seen, it had small boney spikes on its limbs.

Almas glanced at the Lich Lord but he didn't seem to have noticed or sensed anything. It had worked! He had used necromancy using bardic magic! With a thought he sent the little undead creature scurrying into the bushes where he had it put one of its own little bone spikes into the ground and with another flash a second little undead creature came into being. He had made this one slightly different. He had it spread out its leafy wings and it flew up and over the wall. He could now see the battle through the eyes of his creation. The flaming whirlwind was now gone and the undead army was assaulting a wall that Lord Mason's people seemed to have made from shields. Lord Teanas was there but he couldn't see his father or any of his other family members.

Almas continued flooding the area with feelings of power, but he made it a feeling of drunk power and added a bit of recklessness into it. Hopefully no one would notice and it would help the defenders.

Almas almost stopped playing when a bird suddenly landed on his shoulders and startled him but he managed to hit his notes and keep his spells going. At the same time another bird landed on the city wall next to his flying undead creature. Ulec was watching him and saw what he was doing. The bird on the wall flapped its wing in a signal asking him what he was doing. Turning his head to the bird on his shoulder Almas whispered, "This is me. Please trust me."

Both birds fluttered off. Ulec would be watching, but thankfully didn't seem to be planning on interfering for now. Almas sent his own creature down to the garbage pile he had used to make the undead bull—he was going to need more help.

Chapter 4

"We need to break through their shield wall!"

"Bring in our cavalry, our mounts should be able to break through that wall without any problems."

"Are you alright? You seem to be a little bit slow. Maybe I should tell the boy to stop."

"I have never felt better, leave the boy be. With his bard powers I feel more powerful than I have ever felt before."

"I don't think we should be trusting him to—"

"I said leave him be. Take care of getting the cavalry ready for their attack!"

"I CAN'T FIND ALMAS!"

Izybel was frantic when she found Gidon amiss the turmoil of the evacuation. Creetan, Cady and Giddy were all right behind her. All around them people were moving; soldiers loading the old, young and infirm into war wagons as mammoths were hitched to them. Others were searching for missing loved ones in the crowd while others headed to the rear city exit. Gidon took a deep breath, facing an army of undead would be easier than this.

"He was with Ulec when the battle began. I'm not sure where they are now but Lord Teanas says Ulec is still with him and they are safe for now."

"We need to find him!"

"The gates are breached; Lord Mason is holding them at the plaza but he could be overrun at any moment. We need to move these people out now!"

Izybel's face was a mask of confliction; her duty to her people at odds with her need to have her children safe. Just as with Gidon, what she could do, won over what she wanted to do.

"You see to the rear of the evacuation, I'll take point."

"Just be careful," Gidon admonished.

"You find our son. Take Cree with you," Izybel responded and then herded Giddy and Cady away.

"Now what?" Creetan asked his father.

"We make sure no one is left behind. Come on."

THE UNDEAD WERE PULLING back. Teanas wondered what they were up to. So far, their makeshift wall was holding but they were pulling back far too soon for them to be giving up. That's when their mounted troops arrived.

"What in Mundial's name are those?" Lord Mason exclaimed.

A line of Kadus Knights had appeared riding on top of massive bears.

"Bear Lords," Teanas muttered.

"I think we're about to get ran over as if we aren't even here,"

Lord Mason said as he gave a hand signal to the rear. Instantly the men began removing the supports for their wall and took positions to take down the wall.

The mounted knights began to charge and Lord Mason motioned Teanas to step down from the benches which were taken away. Ballista from the roofs opened fired.

"What are you planning?" Teanas asked.

"Their animal lords are big. Ours are bigger." With another hand signal a line of Lord Mason's war mammoths came into view behind them. The beasts walked side by side with only just enough room for a man to stand with his back pressed against the wall of the buildings on either side of the line of mammoths. Men scurried to get out of the way and just moments before the two mounted forces met at the shield wall Lord Mason shouted an order and the men manning the wall disconnected their shields and moved out of the way just as the mammoths reached them. A moment later the two opposing forces met.

The first Mammoth lowered its head and scooped up the first mounted bear with its tusks and tossed it to the side to be trampled by another mammoth. As they entered the plaza the men in the baskets began shooting arrows from their bows and explosive jars from their slings.

As soon as the mammoths were past, the soldiers formed ranks in a defensive position. There would be no time to reform their wall.

"What about your mammoths?" Teanas asked as he took a forward position with Lord Mason and watched the mammoths disappear behind the boulder.

"Either they will break through and escape or they won't.

The men knew the risks."

There was no time for more discussion as the undead slammed into their lines yet again.

CREETAN'S WORLD WAS confusion. He had been awakened suddenly by the horns sounding the alarm only to immediately find both Almas and Ulec were gone. Where the two could have wandered off too after the day they had had was beyond him. Then having to convince his frantic mother that he had no idea where they had gone. Then his father had told them the pair had gotten themselves stuck on the other side of the enemy force. What was going on?

He was now with his father helping people flee towards the rear of the city, helping some onto war wagons, ordering others to abandon bulky objects that would do nothing but slow down their escape. Meanwhile the sound of clanging swords could now be heard coming from the front of the city.

His father heard it also.

"Come on, we need to see how bad off things are."

Creetan followed his father, his Uncle Jarad, and a few other of his father's men to the front of the city. The narrow entrance to the city proper from the outer plaza had been turned into a kill zone by Lord Mason and his men. Arrows and exploding jars rained down from the rooftops of the buildings while the guards cut down anything that made it pass the deadly hail.

As they approached the rear ranks, they passed a row of pillars that seemed to have risen from beneath cobblestones. A man was on the ground with his head in a hole where one of the pillars seemed to have failed to rise and was tinkering with something.

Meanwhile Creetan's father drew his sword and also raised his hand and Creetan saw a glowing golden shield appear between a guard on the ground and a revenant that was about to overcome him. The guard regained his footing immediately and rejoined the fight. Lord Mason and Lord Teanas appeared from the front ranks covered in the sweat of battle and Lord Mason addressed his father.

"We will have to fall back; we were going to create another firewall but one of our fire screws is jammed. If we can't fix it there will be a gap in the flames, they will be able to pass through."

As Creetan's father gave Lord Mason a brief update on the evacuation a bird landed on Teanas' shoulder and started chirping in his ear. After his father had given his update Lord Teanas spoke as the bird flew away.

"Ulec says he thinks that Almas may have found a way to keep the undead army from pursuing us past the rear city gates."

"Did your bird friend happen to tell you how he was planning to do that?" Jarad asked.

"No, but I wouldn't underestimate either of those boys. If they think they found a way then I would consider their success a good possibility," Lord Teanas responded. There was something in his voice Creetan hadn't seen before. He almost seemed to be trying to convince himself.

"If they did succeed then the undead would have to march south to Fireforge's Pass," Lord Mason murmured.

"How many settlements would be in their path?" Gidon

asked.

"Several small towns and villages before getting to Fireforge itself."

"Is Beaver Dam along the way?" Gidon asked.

"Yes, why?" Lord Mason asked.

"The people of Jaspen evacuated there before the city fell."

Lord Mason gave Creetan's father an incredulous look and asked, "How did you get them there? Even if you could pass through the forest that would take several days."

"I won't speak of how it was done on a battle field, but Ulec assured me they made it there. They will have to be warned."

Creetan couldn't keep quiet any longer, he had to speak up, "What about Almas?"

All the men looked to him so he continued, "He and Ulec are out there; what are you going to do about them?"

"Creetan," his father began," Things are complicated. Don't think for a moment that every fiber of my being isn't screaming at me to go out and fight my way to your brother, but I not only can't fight my way through an army but I have thousands of lives depending on me. I will do everything I can but for the moment we have to trust Ulec to watch over him."

"That's it? He's trying to save us but all we do for him is hope an elvish boy can protect him from an army?" Creetan couldn't believe what he was hearing, his brother was out there and not even his own father was going to do anything!

"Creetan, there is more going on here than you know about," his father started, " and we don't have time to discuss it, there is a battle going on!"

At that moment someone called from the ranks of defenders," My Lords, the enemy is regrouping! "

"I must go," Lord Mason said and turned to Lord Teanas and said, "Thank you for your assistance but I believe you will be of more benefit to my people if you go with Lord Aguerius." Then without another word he was back into the fight.

"We have to go too son," Creetan's father spoke with a gentler tone.

Creetan thought back to just that morning when Almas had brought Lord Mason and his men to save them, he also thought about the battle a few days earlier when Almas had used his bardic abilities to steady his shaking hand and focus his panicked mind. His brother had saved him twice; he couldn't walk away.

"I'm going after him."

His father who had already turned to leave stopped cold and faced his oldest son.

"What was that?"

"If you're not going to do anything then I will. I'm going after him."

Lord Teanas quickly spoke before Creetan's father had the chance to respond, "That won't be necessary, I will go after the boys."

"You have a way out of the city past them?" Gidon asked with raised eyebrows.

"There is a tunnel I can use."

"I'm going with him," Creetan quickly spoke, "He shouldn't go alone. I can help."

His father didn't say anything for a moment, he just stared at his son, then, to Creetan's shock, he reached out and snapped his family crests from around his neck, the crests that identified him as his parent's son, and said, "If you go then you will not be needing this."

Then before Creetan could react his father removed his own crest and placed it over Creetan's head.

"This one will serve you much better. With this I recognize you has my heir. With this crest you will have all my titles, authority and responsibilities; your words will be my words, your acts will be my acts."

Creetan didn't speak, he could only stare in complete shock while his father continued, "Go with Lord Teanas to Beaver Dam and see to our people's safety there. Your authority will help you both in finding and helping Almas and in assisting the people down there that will find themselves in the Lich Lords path."

Looking to Teanas he addressed the Elf Lord, "Will you take him with you?"

"Yes, his authority will be of great assistance in working with your people."

"Then it is time to go, take this," Gidon removed his bow from his shoulder and handed it to Creetan, "This is a special bow, it can protect you, Lord Teanas will explain. Now go before I realize what I'm doing and change my mind."

His father then held him by his shoulders for just a moment before turning around and walked briskly away followed by his men; his Uncle Jarad gave him a grin and said, "Good luck *Lord* Aguerius," before turning and following the others.

"Come, we must be off," Lord Teanas spoke motioning for him to follow.

Creetan followed, wondering just what he was getting himself into.

GREYSEN CURSED HIMSELF; he had designed these flame screws and it was now of all times he found a flaw in those designs. When he had tried to raise the screw to get it ready to use, it had failed to rise. One of the metal pegs had come loose and had wedged itself just right in the machinery so that it couldn't deploy. He had removed a panel to try to remove it but he couldn't quite reach it. He tried dislodging it by hitting it with whatever tool he could reach it with, but so far it would not budge. He didn't have time to disassemble the whole thing to reach it so he kept trying to pound it out with the top of his hammer.

Around him he could hear guards begin to retreat past him; he was running out of time. He heard Lord Mason's voice above him, "Greysen! We have to go now!"

"I just need one more minute!"

"One minute!" Lord Mason promised. The sounds of fighting were right behind him, he didn't dare look up to see what was happening he just kept pounding. It was at that moment something crawled past him into the hole. It was...well, he wasn't sure what it was, it looked like some small creature that had been put together from small bones, tree, and plant clippings. But the small spikes coming out of what the thing was using for legs clearly marked it as undead.

He was about to smash it when the thing put one of its spikes into a wooden panel; there was a flash of darkness and a section of the panel had disappeared. He noticed two things at that moment, the first was that the sound of fighting behind him had ceased; he was out of time. The second thing was with part of the panel missing he now had a much better angle to hit the wedged piece of metal from. He gave the hammer one last swing with all he had left and with a snap the fire screw shot up out of the ground. He had done it!

A shadow appeared on the screw taking the form of a revenant raising a sword above him. Greysen smiled, his life for the life of hundreds wasn't a bad trade. He extended his hand toward the switch to start the screw. It was out of reach but he had built this device, he could feel his connection to it; with a little push from magic the switch moved and all the screws in the row began to spin. Then there was a brief flash of heat followed by nothing as flames consumed everything.

THE FLAMES FROM THE row of spinning screws ignited the buildings on either side creating a massive wall of flames that burned solid for an hour giving the defenders time to clear the city.

Gidon watched as guards helped the last of the people out of the gates and into the narrow road passing between two solid rock faces.

"Are there any people left in there?" Gidon asked.

"None we can find my lord."

"And Lord Mason?"

"He was last seen guarding Graysen as he worked on the fire screws. That was moments before they turned on; he hasn't been seen since," the guard responded sadly.

Gidon cursed himself. He should have been there.

"Alright let's go," he ordered his men. He mounted his

forest dragon as the others mounted their own dragons and horses. They then rode to a spot as far from the gates as they could and still be able to see them.

He watched as more and more plumes of smoke appeared closer and closer over the city. Then he heard pounding at the gates they had closed and barred as they left. Soon the gates were broken down and the undead army began passing through.

Gidon sighed in disappointment. He didn't know what the Lich Lords had done to his son, but when Ulec had sent the message that Almas was trying to stop the undead from pursuing them, he couldn't help but hope; but here they were, still coming. Now he would need to set up ambushes all along the way to slow the enemy down.

His thoughts were interrupted by what sounded like an extremely loud clash of thunder, only the rumbling wasn't fading, in fact it seemed to be growing louder.

"Look up there!" Someone shouted.

Gidon saw it. A huge rockslide coming down both cliffs right above the undead army. He caught a glimpse of the army retreating back to the city before falling dust and debris blocked his view.

It seemed to take forever for the dust to clear enough to reveal the massive pile of large boulders and rocks blocking the passage. It would take months to clear the passage enough to pass an army through now.

Gidon took in a breath and fought back a sob of relief. Maybe there was hope after all. For them, and for his missing son.

ALMAS DROPPED HIS BONE flute and collapsed onto his back as the lich near him cried out in dismay. Even from the front gates of the city the landslide was visible.

Deleta was the first to speak, "They rigged the cliffs to collapse and block pursuit!"

"He will not escape us that easily, I swear every last one of them will suffer," the undead monster swore as he stomped off.

Almas was only vaguely aware of this. He couldn't believe it had worked. He had sent some of his undead creeps, as he had started calling his little creations in his head, up to the top of the cliff and began building up as much magic as he could. Once the undead army began moving into the passage, he used these creeps to turn all the trees and plants along the edge of the cliff into undead minions and used their root systems to break up the rocks and soil and start the rockslide. It had taken everything he had but it had worked! For now, at least, his family was safe.

He didn't get much time to bask in his victory as he suddenly felt hands grab him by his shirt and lift him off the ground. In an instant his feet were dangling over a foot off the ground and he was face to face with a very angry Deleta.

"Don't think you fooled me for a moment with that spell you cast with that song. The only reason you're still alive are Lord Lich-El's orders, but if you ever try to deceive me like that again you will be sorry."

Almas took his full undead form and looking Deleta in the eye said, "You think you can do more to me than has already been done? If you want to kill me then trust me when I say I would welcome it!"

Deleta dropped Almas in surprise. Almas collapsed back down to a sitting position but never broke eye contact with the Kadus Knight. Deleta's expression stayed surprised for a few moments before softening for just an instant to a look of pity. But after that instant it was replaced once again by cold hate.

"Well, I'm afraid you're going to have to get used to your new life, apparently there are plans for you. Welcome to the service of Lich-El.

Chapter 5

"They blocked the pass with a landslide?"

"Yes, we will have to bring our army back to camp for now. Unless you can create a gate to the other side of the landslide?"

"By the time I get a revenant over the slide, it won't matter. We can start raiding nearby villages and towns to build up our strength."

"Very well, send out your runners and I will see to getting the army ready to pass through your gate back to camp."

THE LICH LORD IN CHARGE was angry. Almas saw that as a good thing. Especially when he learned that he was angry at the few number of prisoners and dead from the battle. Most of the few prisoners taken were surviving guards, and the dead didn't nearly come close to the number of revenants lost invading the city.

Deleta was also angry but Almas could tell he was also a bit disturbed at seeing his father's 12-year-old namesake in the form of an undead lich. Almas made it a point to stay in that form and let him see exactly what the creatures he was serving did to those with the last name Aguerius.

"Come with me boy!" The Lich Lord in charge commanded him after returning from organizing the removal of the undead army back to their new base camp.

Almas responded by making a rather rude face at the creature. He had no order to obey this particular monster.

"Get up and do as Trumion says!" Deleta ordered.

Okay, now he did have to listen to that particular monster. He got up and followed the even angrier lich.

"By Lich-El's command you are to help us come up with optional battle plans. Why he thinks a child has any valuable insight on war is beyond me."

"I wouldn't expect too much, I have a cursed wound on my shoulder and should be dying of infection in a few days."

"I wouldn't be so sure about that," Trumion said with a wicked grin, "In your undead form your regeneration powers will wipe out any infection. You also have no blood flowing so as long as we make sure you don't spend too long in your human form, I think you will be just fine."

Almas realized the lich was probably right. He couldn't feel the pain he had had in his shoulder since taking Ulec's curse on himself. So much for that hope.

Almas was led with Deleta into a tent with a table covered in maps. The lich, Trumion continued, "With the pass blocked we will have to attack towns and cities to the north and south. We will give you what information we have on the towns and cities that will be in our path. You will make the best plans you can in taking these cities and we will see if you are worth the trouble Lord Lich-El thinks you are."

"North *and* south. You won't be attacking in just one direction?" Almas asked.

"No, we will send out scouts to all the cities and use gate travel to focus our forces in the attack."

Almas looked at the map and the names of villages, towns, and cities in the path of the undead horde. How could he make plans for attacking them? There were thousands of people in towns and cities that would soon come in range of an undead attack. To his absolute horror he realized part of his mind was already working out attack plans.

He was relieved for the distraction when another Lich-Lord came in and said, "Lord Trumion, forgive me but one of our prisoners says he has information that he will only give to you."

"Who is this prisoner?"

"It is the Lord of this city."

"Let him in but make sure he is unarmed."

After a moment Lord Mason was brought in, although it took a moment for Almas to recognize him. His clothes were shredded and he looked to be a bloody mess. Almas stared at him in horror as Lord Mason looked around the room, his eyes landing on Almas who realized he was in his undead form. Without even thinking he switched back to his human form, looking away in shame. Lord Mason's city was a wrecked ghost town now because of him.

Aside from being beaten, Lord Mason looked oddly ill and was looking at Almas with sorrowful look.

"So, it is true, they did do something to you."

Almas tried to explain, "I'm so sorry, I couldn't stop myself. I tried... "

Lord Mason said, "No, I'm sorry. I had three exploding jars with me and had a long drink before being captured. I'm afraid I can't put this off any longer. Have to do this where it will do the most good."

Trumion and Deleta both looked confused but Almas understood immediately. He grabbed Deleta by the wrist and shouted "Lookout" as he, without thinking, stepped in front of the Kadus Knight. He felt himself thrown into Deleta as the tent suddenly turned into an expanding fireball and the world went dark.

"Thank goodness I'm finally dead," was the first thing Almas thought to himself.

A familiar voice answered, "Not yet I'm afraid. You're in another dream."

Almas sat up and looked around. In this dream he was in Aguerius Forest and sitting on a log near him was Lord Teanas.

"You were in my last dream. You aren't the real Lord Teanas but you aren't just a dream, are you?"

"No, I'm not just a dream, I'm a fieles."

"What about Lord Mason?"

The fieles shook his head, "He used magic to ignite the explosives he drank. I'm afraid he sacrificed himself to take down a high-ranking Lich Lord. He knew he would have been made a revenant and he didn't want that. He also wanted to hurt the undead army as best as he could."

"How am I still alive? Wait, I think I have this. You're a fieles, one that must have been made from a piece of Lord Teanas' soul, and one of his powers is being fireproof. Let me guess, I have you to blame for my continued existence?"

The fieles nodded, "I was made because Teanas wanted you

to be protected. My name is Fireweaver. He decided not to tell you about me when he gave you the rusica because he suspected the undead had done more to you than we had been told. He wanted me to try to find out what."

"Well, he was a little late. Any bright ideas how I can get out of this situation?"

The fieles Fireweaver shook his head sadly and said, "I'm sorry I don't. But remember, *you* are not responsible for what *they* choose to do."

Almas responded, "What they can do, is use me how they want to hurt whoever they want me to; and now they have your abilities to add to that once they find out about you."

Suddenly Almas began to feel the dream to collapse. He opened his eyes, the first thing he saw was Deleta crouched over him.

"Well, my head really hurts, what hit me...besides a wall of flame?" Almas groaned.

Deleta looked a little conflicted, but he answered, "The blast threw you into me and you hit your head really hard on my armor. You wouldn't wake up till I ordered you into your undead form."

Almas could feel a tingling in his head as the bad bump he got quickly healed. This undead regeneration had its good points, he was already thinking of ways to use that.

"How did you protect us from the fire like that," Deleta demanded.

Almas sighed and answered, "Apparently, my friends snuck a fieles on me. When we touched after the explosion pushed me into you, the protection I had must have extended to you."

"Why did you try to shield me?"

"Besides the fact you're my cousin? I guess you can call it a bad habit. That is how I ended up with a hole in my chest to start off with, a bad habit of trying to protect people."

By now Kadus Knights and a few revenants from other lich lords could be seen approaching. Deleta seemed to think a moment and said, "They will take your fieles if they know about it. Tell them we were on the edge of the blast, you shielded me and regenerated already from the burns."

Almas' eyes widened in surprise. "You're helping me?"

"Lich-el demands I pay all debts of honor. Besides, a fieles like that might come in handy, but not if it is in the hands of Tornal or any of the other lich lords besides Lord Lich-El.

"I won't argue with that." Almas surveyed the destruction around them and tried not to think about Lord Mason. By now Kadus Knights were arriving. Deleta waved them off when they asked him if he was alright.

Deleta led Almas away from the devastation. Almas asked as he followed, "So.....who do we need to let know that they just got a promotion; now that Trumion is a pile of ash?"

"That would be me," came a familiar voice, one that Almas had hoped he would never hear again. Looking up ahead he saw Tornal grinning at him.

Almas didn't even hesitate, not wanting to give anyone a chance to order him to stop. He just pointed his right hand straight at Tornal, the one who had made him into the monster he now was.

Tornal must have felt Almas draw in all the surrounding death energy because his sinister grin vanished and he started to move aside.

Almas' right arm vanished in a dark flash, being replaced

by a long bone spear that caught the moving Tornal in his shoulder, right at the base of the arm. Before Almas could do anything else Deleta called out, "Almas! Stop!"

The bone spear, that had been Almas' arm, crumbled into dust as did Tornal's arm from the point the bone spear had struck him.

Almas was the first to speak, "Well, I really thought that would hurt a lot. It didn't hurt at all. That will be good to know once my arm regenerates."

Tornal, his face a mask of fury, sputtered, "How dare you...I am your master."

Almas smiled, "You kinda forgot to order me not to try to kill you, so you know I had to try. Guess I need to work on my aim."

"You are as of now forbidden to attack or hurt any lich lord," Tornal ordered, glaring at Almas.

"Knew that order would come eventually," Almas said sadly.

"What did you do? And how?" Asked Deleta.

Almas responded matter-of-factly, "The bone spikes on our arms converts dead things to undead things. Undead things are technically still dead, so I converted my undead arm into an undead bone spear. You guys never put a whole lot of thought into what is possible with your powers have you? Seriously, couldn't Lich-El find anyone with half a brain to join up?

Then without waiting for an answer, Almas changed the subject, "By the way, out of curiosity, Lich-El told my father you were being punished for what you did to me. What was the punishment?"

Tornal answered, "He said you would be my punishment

and I was forbidden to get rid of you. Now we have wasted enough time. You are to come with me and put that supposed brilliance of yours to work on battle plans."

The idea of making planes against his family, friends, and people made Almas feel sick, but he had no choice to obey. He began to follow the Lich Lord along with Deleta but couldn't resist one more jab; after all, he was supposed to be Tornal's punishment. "Bet you I can grow my arm back before you can."

Tornal glared at him while a glance at Deleta showed the Kadus Knight struggling not to laugh.

Chapter 6

"So, the boy is a strategic genius after all."

"Just as Lich-El said. Imagine the plans he could come up with if he was doing it willingly."

"I hope you are not becoming fond of him. Just remember he belongs to me, and don't think I will tolerate that annoying brat for one moment past the second he stops being useful to me."

"You might have turned him into what he is now but don't forget he belongs to Lich-El. Besides, he is only an annoying brat to you. He has taken his role of being your punishment very seriously."

"And just where is our beloved Lord Lich-El? No one has seen him since the battle of Jaspen."

"I don't care where he is, so long as he is keeping Lady Alixia there, and not here."

CREETAN FOLLOWED LORD Teanas through yet another destroyed village. The undead army so far was moving rapidly south and Creetan was unsure if they would make it to Beaver Dam before them. In fact, he was increasingly certain that they wouldn't.

With every wrecked village came survivors. Mostly children that had fled and hidden in woods and fields. Others that had been hidden by parents and not discovered. They had found one of the war mammoths along with two men from its basket that had fought their way through the undead army and had escaped pursuit. They had found a useable war wagon near one of the ruined villages and were using it to move survivors.

Where to take them was the problem. He couldn't keep following the undead army with them. He would only be delivering these people to the very doom they had just escaped. Yet he had to get to Beaver Dam as he promised his father, and he needed to find Almas.

"If you head south-east from here you might be able to get the refugees out of undead controlled lands and then send them on to the Yucaipa Province. If you then hurry to the south-west you might be able to get past the undead army and beat them to Beaver Dam."

It was the fieles, Sacred Knight, which had spoken directly to his mind. It would seem that during the War of Destruction, Lord Morin Aguerius had allowed a fieles to be created from a piece of his soul. The fieles had then been passed down the Paladin's line. His advice had so far been greatly helpful.

"They are moving so quickly. Do you really think we can overtake them by going so far around them?" Creetan asked.

"You will never overtake them with these people with you, nor could you protect them if you did."

"Creetan!"

Creetan looked to the source of the voice that had called his name. It was Teanas. The elf moved ahead of him as he had been deep in thought and now approached him quickly.

"We have six more survivors," Teanas said.

Six more people that Creetan was responsible for. How did his father do it? How could he take responsibility for an entire province without his insides twisting up or going crazy?

"Sacred Knight thinks we should head towards the Yucaipa Province and send all the survivors there once we are clear of the undead. Then try for Beaver Dam," Creetan said.

"We would get there too late," another voice stated.

Creetan whirled around to see another familiar face, "Ulec! Where have you been?"

"Making friends with the local animals and trying to keep track of Almas."

"You know where he is?" Creetan asked hopefully.

"It took a little while, but yes, they have him at a hidden base up in the mountains. Most of their army stays there. They only leave when one of Tornal's scouts reaches a village or town, he just opens a gate, and the Lich's armies attack."

"So that is how they are moving so fast," Teanas said.

"Yes, it is," confirmed Ulec, "That's the bad news. The good news is that there are only a few scouts between here and Beaver Dam. If we hurry, we might be able to get there first."

"Why do you look like you have more bad news?" Creetan asked.

"Because I do. The Lich Lords have been having Almas make the battle plans."

"What? He's twelve!" Creetan exclaimed.

"Yes," Teanas said gravely, "but he is also brilliant in strategy, even more so than your father. Even with his lack of experience, he would be the undead's greatest asset."

"But he would never help them. He would find ways to sabotage their plans," Creetan argued.

"And he has been trying," Ulec answered, "But when he is ordered to give his best plan, he has no choice but to give them his best plan. The curse he is under doesn't allow him to do differently."

"So, if you know where he is, why haven't you rescued him? Get him out of there so they can't use him!"

"I would if I could. He is under orders. I'd have to fight him to get him out of there, how would he feel about that? And even if I did get him out, he would still be under their control. Remember what happened to Debigroc? He feels every death in that city is his fault. Any place we take him we risk having the same thing happen," Ulec said defending himself.

Creetan sighed in frustration. He needed to do something for his brother. But even if he knew what to do, how could he do it when he had to take care of so many people.

"Do you really think we can get these people safely to Beaver Dam?"

Ulec nodded.

"Let's hurry than."

"There is something else," Ulec said turning to look at his father, Almas knows about the fieles you snuck on him. The one made from a piece of your soul. When were you going to tell me my rusica is a fieles too?"

To make his point he extended his hand and, in a flash of light, his rusica turned into a sword. "With a piece of Mother's soul, it works just like your ring, Mimic."

Lord Teanas winced and said, "Not telling you was your mother's condition in having them made. She was hoping to learn more about what happened to Almas while he was with the undead. I only wanted extra protection for both of you."

"Well, you will be happy to know it has already saved his life as well as Deleta's. Let's just hope the Lich Lords don't find out he has an item that makes the wearer fire proof and able to control fire."

THE UNDEAD ARMY WAS just about how Almas had always pictured it. They were...well...dead. Even the Lich Lords lacked just about any kind of personality.

It was the Kadus Knights that surprised him. He was expecting the living servants of the undead to be the worst people humanity had to offer. Men filled with everlasting hate for the rest of mankind. It was true that a few of the Kadus Knights were like that, but he was shocked, not to mention a little unsettled, to find that most of them seemed to be friendly.

What surprised him the most was the fact that there weren't just warriors in the camp...there were families. When Almas had first been to the human part of the war camp, he had been horrified at seeing children of all ages present. What kind of monsters took children with them on a campaign of murder?

After so many days being forced to tag along with the leader of the Kadus Knights, something was starting to tell him that these humans weren't anything like he had assumed them to be. At the moment, that something was Kade.

Kade was a boy about the same age as Almas, who seemed to have an endless supply of questions. His father was second in command of the Kadus Knights despite being over a decade older than Deleta.

"So, is it true that the Guardian Spirit of Aguerius Forest is an elf kid?" The boy asked him as he was writing out another battle plan for Tornal. The boy had slipped into the tent and had been hurling questions at him. Almas had considered telling him to go away but he hoped that maybe the boy would distract him and lower the quality of his work. He could tell that it wasn't working even as he responded to Kade's question.

"You mean Ulec? You know about him?"

"Of course, all the survivors from the battle against High Lord Aguerius speak about the two elves, one that controls fire and another that controls the very forest itself, oh and they talk about the elvish lady that can kick blasts of energy at people; I hear she is almost as strong as Lich-El."

Kicks blasts of energy? He must have heard about when Lady Alixia killed the lich that almost had taken them all prisoner at Demon Mountain. Lady Alixia had taken the form of some other elf and had tapped her toe on the ground. A small crack had shot out to the lich and he had disappeared in a pillar of energy that had erupted from the ground.

"That was Lady Alixia, she is strong but I think Ulec might be even more powerful, at least he will be if he isn't already," Almas said.

"We had always heard that there was a great power that protected the Sacred Forest of Mundial but we never guessed it was an elvish boy. My father says he watched the boy take out the entire force that tried to follow your people into Aguerius Forest with ants. He was sure he was a dead man before Deleta thought of a way to escape the trap."

THE NECROMANCER

Almas was feeling extremely awkward. He hadn't thought much about the Kadus Knights that had fallen in the battles he had seen, after all, they were the evil servants of the Lich Lords, weren't they? Now he was starting to wonder; how many children had lost parents during these battles? And what kind of parents were they?

He had seen Kade training with his father. It reminded him of watching his own father training with Creetan. Kade's father seemed to be a really good one. It was really hard to keep hating your enemy when you find out so many of them are people just like you. And here Almas was making battle plans that would result in so many deaths of these people and in the deaths of so many of his own.

"So, what is he like?" Kade asked pulling Almas from his thoughts.

"Who? Ulec? He's well...Ulec. He's really smart and really fast and is the best weapons master I know except maybe his father. He's kinda quiet around people he doesn't know well. He's been my best friend for over four years now."

"Do you think I could meet him some time? Everyone says I have the quickest knife fighting skills of all the apprentices. Maybe we could dual?"

"You do realize you are on opposite sides of a war, don't you? I'm afraid a dual against Ulec would leave you not only defeated but likely dead."

"Being killed by the best would be a glorious death. Defeating the best would be glorious beyond compare."

Okay, while Kadus Knights were admittedly human, they were also weird. With the current battle plan finished it was his turn to ask some questions.

"So, where did the Kadus Knights come from? We all thought that they were made up of fugitives from the Yucaipan Kingdom, but I get the feeling that isn't true."

Kade answered, "Many of our people are ones that have fled from the oppression of the Lords of your people. But many of us are descended from Chaos Knights. They were Snipies' Honor Guard. In the early days of the War of Destruction Snipies tried to end the war by attacking Destruction's Sacred Forest far to the east of here. It was the final battle between Kaynarian Sky Chariots, they all destroyed each other and crashed to the ground. Those that survived continued the fight on the ground. In the end we won. With the Sky Chariots gone there was no way to rejoin the war or even let Snipies know there were survivors. He and the other gods were too busy with the war to look for any.

"After they found out that Snipies had been killed in the final battle they renamed themselves Kadus Knights after the man they appointed their leader."

"How did you end up working for the undead?" Almas asked.

"About 50 years ago the village we had made was attacked by demons. Lich-El came and saved them. We have had an honor debt to him ever since," Kade answered.

"And how did my cousin become your leader?"

Kade shrugged, "He's the best warrior. Lich-El brought him to us when his father died and we adopted him as one of us. When he became our greatest warrior, he earned the right to lead. Hey, do you want to have dinner with my family?"

"You do realize I'm here against my will and if I ever get free of this curse, we'll be enemies trying to kill each other, don't you?" Almas asked.

"If you get free of your curse then we can always fight to the death. Till then, you should come have dinner with us. My parents will be going with the troops attacking Beaver Dam tomorrow, I want you to meet them before they go."

"As much as fun as having dinner with some of my captors sounds, I need to get these plans to Deleta." Almas answered dryly.

"Okay," Kade responded cheerfully, "Maybe when they get back."

Almas watched Kade leave, the boy's enthusiasm not suffering any apparent loss. These Kadus Knights were really weird.

"I am sure they find you equally as weird. Do not forget they have been taught since their earliest childhood different values than you. If they are descended from survivors of Snipies' honor guard, then they will reflect his values, not all of which are bad." The voice of the fieles on his hand said, after obviously reading his thoughts.

Almas responded with a question, *"So you think that story is true?"*

The answer came after a moment of waiting, *"I believe it is very possible. Most of Snipies forces were lost in the battle Kade mentioned, and the Knights do seem to reflect Snipies' influence. Their focus on bravery, honor, and glory and their putting a lesser importance on the value of life whether it is their own or that of others, being the best evidence. The war gave us little time to search for survivors after any of the battles."*

"Just keep reminding me that they are trying to kill my family if I start liking them too much".

Almas took the battle plans he finished to Deleta. Tornal preferred not to deal with Almas since he made sure to take his role as Tornal's punishment to the full extent he knew how. So, he spent most of his time with Deleta, who wasn't so bad ever since Almas saved his life.

Almas arrived at Deleta's tent and went in. "More battle plans his Royal pain in-"

Tornal was in the tent so Almas had to stop speaking abruptly. Not that he cared if Tornal heard him, but because Tornal had ordered him to never speak in his presence. So, once he saw Tornal, the curse effectively gagged him. As if Almas needed to speak to find ways to pester a Lich Lord.

Almas handed the battle plans to Deleta and then stretched his arms out with a big yawn making sure to exaggerate wiggling all his fingers, especially the ones that had already grown back. Tornal was still working on regenerating his own fingers. Almas smirked at the lich.

Tornal glared at him a moment before speaking. "You will come with me. You will be going with us on our attack on Beaver Dam and we have things to discuss."

Almas didn't say anything...he couldn't if he had wanted to, but he was sure his surprise showed on his face. He hadn't participated in any battle since he had been forced to open the gate at Debigroc.

Tornal left the tent and Almas followed. Was that a pitying look Deleta gave him right before he left the tent?

They walked through the tents of the Kadus Knights and stopped at the grounds they had been using for training. Kade was there practicing combat skills with his father.

Both he and his father were practicing with the same odd

looking knifes he had seen them practice with before. The blades didn't come straight out of the handles but at an angle. The handles were also shaped strangely being in a similar shape as the blades, just not sharpened.

As before when he had watched them practice, Almas couldn't help but be a little nervous. When his father had taught sword fighting to Creetan they had used dull practice weapons; Kade and his father were using real weapons and at the speed they were sparring, Almas was sure someone was going to lose a hand.

At one point, Kade took a step back and threw one his knifes. Almas always found this part interesting because he didn't throw it at his father but to the side and as he attacked his father with his other knife, the spinning odd-looking knife, rather than keep going the direction it was thrown, it moved in an arc around to the back of his father till it was about to strike him from behind. At the same time Kade lunged at his father forcing him to deal with an attack from both in front and behind him both together. His father blocked Kade's thrust with the knife in one hand and deflected the thrown knife with the knife in his other hand.

The deflected knife shot upward and then suddenly arced downward right back to Kade's empty hand.

"Did you see what happened there?" Tornal asked and then quickly added, "You may answer the questions."

"The weird knife moved in an arc by itself but after it was deflected Kade used magic to change its direction to bring it back to his hand," Almas responded.

"Can you see his magic ability?"

"Yes."

"Describe it," Tornal ordered.

"It seems to grow a little each time he uses it."

"How does it compare to the abilities your elf friends have or like your father's paladin abilities?"

"It is a lot weaker and doesn't seem as stable. It becomes stronger as it is used and weakens when it isn't. My father's paladin abilities are always the same, only the magic put into it changes," Almas answered.

Tornal nodded, "I have found there are two types of magic abilities; talents and gifts. Talents are abilities that come by study and practice. They grow as you build them but they can also be lost if neglected. Gifts are abilities that one is born with or given, such as your father's paladin abilities or Lady Alixia's ability to take the form of those she comes in contact with. Those abilities are always there regardless of practice or effort."

Tornal stopped watching the father and son as they practiced and faced Almas as he said, "When I gave you the powers of undeath I also gave you the ability to take these gifts and talents from others and also the ability to give what you take to others, just as you took that curse from your friend and took it on yourself."

Tornal smiled and patted Almas' shoulder where the cursed wound that had once been on Ulec's shoulder was now slowly bleeding underneath his own bandages. The contact really hurt but Almas didn't even flinch; he was becoming use to the pain.

Lucky for him it only affected him while in his human form. While undead the wound stopped bleeding and his regenerative abilities wiped out any growing infection before it became a problem. In other words, there was little threat of this curse killing him like it had nearly done to Ulec unless he spent too long in his human form.

Almas wanted to ask Tornal where he was going with all this but he couldn't and was also a little afraid he knew the answer. Tornal didn't make him wait.

"Tomorrow during the battle, you will help me by taking abilities from our enemies and then give them to me."

Almas wanted to ask why Tornal didn't give himself the power to steal abilities and let him go home, but he couldn't due to the gag order. His fieles answered his question for him.

"He said you were an experiment. He would need to make sure everything turns out as he wants before doing it to himself."

"So why keep me around, if he knows it works, he could give himself the abilities and get rid of me."

"I'm not sure. It might be Lich-El has ordered him to keep you around or he hasn't finished his experiment or perhaps for some reason he cannot repeat it."

"I'll add that to my list of things to find out."

Meanwhile Kade's practice session had ended and while his father left, the curly haired boy came up to his audience.

"Hi Almas, are you still under the gag order with Tornal around?"

Silence from Almas was his answer. Tornal answered him instead, "Go home boy, we have no time for you, we have a battle to prepare for."

Kade ignored the lich lord and continued speaking to Almas, "Since you can't speak, would you like me to pester Stubby for you?"

Was this kid crazy? Almas vigorously shook his head no, but Kade—being Kade—ignored it and directed his next words to Tornal, "Almas says he hates you and hopes you get turned to ash really soon."

Yes...Kade was most definitely crazy. Tornal glared as he spoke, "I would recommend you go home now boy or I can guarantee you will never go home again."

Kade smiled, "That would violate the terms of our alliance."

"Only if it can be proven it was me. Trust me I would make sure your disappearance would forever be a mystery. I'm very good at such things."

The boy and the lich stared at each other for, what felt to Almas, an extremely long and tense moment, which was probably in reality just a few moments before Tornal said, "I haven't the time to deal with nuisances like you. I have a battle to prepare for. But I wouldn't expect to grow much older if I were you." And with that he stormed away.

Once Tornal was gone Almas got his voice back. "Are you completely crazy? Tornal is going to kill you and he will probably use me to do it!"

Kade shrugged, "Everyone hates him. Most of us wish he would hurry up and betray Lich-El like we all know he is planning to; that way we could be done with him. But he won't any time soon. He would lose the Kadus Knights as allies if he did and he still needs us. Their revenants aren't powerful enough; by themselves they lose far more revenants than they create. Without us they would need to enter the battle themselves, and most of them, Tornal included, are too cowardly for that."

"What if they find out there is a better way to create an undead army than making revenants from dead humans? How much will you and the rest of your people be worth than?"

"Better than revenants?" Kade asked with a hint of

confusion on his face and then suddenly breaking out in a huge grin, "You already figured something out! You've been the Necromancer for how long? And you have already figured out something they haven't in the hundred years they've been doing this? You have to tell me about it."

"Necromancer?" Almas asked confused.

Kade explained, "Well, you aren't really a lich, but not human anymore either. Some of the knights have started referring to you as the Necromancer. Anyway, what did you figure out?

Almas wasn't sure about this new title of his and was about to tell Kade to go away when he heard a voice in his head say, *"Go ahead and show him."*

"If the Lich Lords hear about the creeps I learned to make, they will win this war and kill everyone in no time," Almas argued with the Fieles. So far Almas had found enough leeway in his orders in making battle plans to have not revealed what he had done and created at Debigroc.

"It is only a matter of time before they will give you an order that forces you to reveal them. We both know the Lich Lords will betray the Kadus Knights eventually, wouldn't it be nice if we could somehow use them against the undead when that happens?"

There could be something to that. The more he learned about the Kadus Knights the more he began to believe that, as a people, they weren't evil. They were certainly strange, but not evil.

Almas took his undead form and broke off one of his bone spikes and told Kade to watch. He pushed some dead leaves and twigs together into a pile with his foot and put the bone spike into the ground. In a flash of darkness, the bone spike and pile vanished and a small undead creature took its place. It looked like some kind of huge bug that could pass itself off as part of a plant. It had a leafy body and legs like twigs. It also had two crab like pincers.

Kade looked at it in wonder and exclaimed, "That is amazing. How sharp are those claws?"

"Cut your finger right off, go ahead and stick one of yours in and see, then we can call you stubby like you did to Tornal."

"No thanks, I don't have a grow-back option on mine like you do...are those small little bone spikes on it? They aren't also poisonous, are they? "Kade asked.

"Yes, they are, just not as poisonous as these are," Almas answered indicating to the bone spikes going up his arms, "but they will pretty much make a man unable to fight or defend himself. I can also use this one to make more like it, with different weapons and different abilities. I call them creeps"

Kade looked around and said, "There are plants, bugs and other animals all around us. You could make an army of these in minutes. You could turn a battle just like that."

"And I could do it without any help from the Kadus Knights," Almas added, "Which is my whole point. If the other Lich Lords learn they can do this, how long do you think it would take for them to decide they don't need your people anymore?"

That thought finally seemed to sober Kade who after thinking a moment shook his head, "Tornal and the other Lich Lords would try to betray us, but Lich-El wouldn't; and even with this new ability they couldn't stand up to him."

"He can't protect you if he isn't here, how long has it been since anyone has seen him?"

"Not since our attack on Jaspen," Kade admitted.

"You can't rely on him to save you if he isn't here. Ally or not, when you are dealing with the likes of Tornal, I think your people may be in as much danger as my own. You might want to think about that. Especially if you insist on pestering him into a fury, which is my job by the way, not yours," Almas said.

Kade seemed to think on that before finally saying, "I'm late for dinner. I'd best be going." He began to step away but stopped suddenly and added, "Be careful tomorrow, it would get real boring around here without you." The boy then headed off towards his family's tent at a jog.

Chapter 7

"Lord Lich-El! You're back!"

"Hello Kade, training by yourself?"

"Everyone is leaving right now to attack Beaver Dam. Where have you been?"

"Delaying a very angry and powerful force from descending upon us in her wrath."

"Lady Alixia?"

"Her too."

DAWN WAS BREAKING AS Creetan and his band of refugees came in sight of Beaver Dam. He was in the basket of the mammoth with Lord Teanas and Ulec.

"It looks like we made it before the undead armies," Creetan observed with relief.

"We should be to the city gates in about 10 minutes, my lord," The driver said.

Creetan glanced at Ulec, who was sitting down in the back of the basket and appeared to be meditating. "Have you found any undead scouts nearby?"

Ulec shook his head as he answered, "Not yet. The animals

around here are very uncooperative. They have never had their minds touched by anyone before. Nearly all the animals push me out of their heads in fear."

"Sounds like you need to start getting out of that forest more," Creetan said teasingly.

"Well, now that my existence isn't really a secret anymore, I might do that," Ulec responded with a faint smile but otherwise not moving from his position of concentration.

Then suddenly he jerked up, his eyes flying open! "I found them!"

"The scouts?" Creetan asked.

"Not just scouts. Their army is coming through a magic gate. They are getting ready to attack the city."

Creetan hesitated a moment before remembering he was the one in charge now. Speaking first to the mammoth's driver he said, "Get us to the city now!" Then turning to one of the guards from Debigroc he ordered, "Signal the city that we are coming and to be on alert for an attack."

The guard immediately put his horn to his lips and began sounding a loud series of trumpeting calls.

Now it was a matter of getting to the city before the attack began. "How much time do you think we have before the attack starts?" Creetan asked Ulec.

"They heard our warning. They are trying to form an attack quickly now, but I think we should make the city before them," Ulec answered.

As they approached the city Creetan noted that the walls and gate weren't nearly as big or strong as those of Debigroc.

Lord Teanas also noticed. "It won't take the undead long to breach those walls. We will need to be prepared for close combat in the streets."

Creetan could see soldiers taking positions on the wall as they approached. The doors however remained closed. Once they were in calling distance Creetan called out. "Open the gates! We have refugees in the war wagon!"

A voice answered from the walls, "They will need to exit the war wagon and enter the city on foot."

"The undead army is about to attack! We don't have time for this!" Creetan answered. Creetan kicked himself. He should have expected such mistrust in a time of war; of course, those protecting the city would need to verify that they were who they claimed.

Luckily, another voice on the wall shouted, "Open the gate, that is Lord Forjad's grandson!"

Immediately the gates began to open and the mammoth and the war wagon quickly entered the city.

Inside the gates, they were quickly surrounded by soldiers. Creetan hurried down from the basket.

"Creetan!" Called the same voice that had ordered the doors opened.

Creetan looked to the voice and smiled as he called back, "Uncle Marpel!"

A man with graying hair and a strange looking staff stepped forward and embraced the young lord. Creetan was surprised to see his uncle. He was High Lord Marpel Vatan, ruler of the now empty Vatan Province. Since the undead had invaded and destroyed the Vatan Province 4 years earlier he had only been around a few times to continue Almas' bard training.

"Uncle Marpel, what are you doing here?" Creetan asked.

"We will talk later my boy," Lord Vatan started then

stopped when he caught sight of Creetan's crest. After a moment's hesitation he continued, "I'm sorry...we will talk later Lord Aguerius, you signaled us that we are about to fall under attack. This is Lord Cordwainer, he is the lord of Beaver Dam. Can you tell us what is going on?"

It was Ulec that spoke startling both men who hadn't noticed the elvish boy approach. "They are gathering to the south. I think they are going to send in Revenants first to try to catch you before you are fully ready to defend the city."

Uncle Marpel stretched out his hand to Ulec, "You must be the famous Ulec, and your father, Lord Teanas. I'm glad to finally meet you both."

First Ulec and then Lord Teanas took his hand in greeting as Lord Cordwainer quickly motioned his soldiers to prepare for the battle.

"I am glad to finally meet you also," Teanas responded. If I might, I believe I could help most on the wall."

"Yes, if you and Creetan will join me, the guards will see your refugees to safety. Ulec, if you would like to go with...where did he go?"

Ulec was nowhere to be seen. Creetan answered his uncle, "You eventually get used to that. He comes and goes as he pleases and always ends up where he is needed most."

"I see—come with me."

Uncle Marpel led them up to the top of the city walls where they took positions on the center of the south walls. Now it was a matter of waiting, although from what Ulec said it wouldn't be much of a wait.

"Is your father alright?" Creetan's uncle asked indicating the new crest that was around his neck.

"Last I saw him he was fine. He was taking refugees from Debigroc and the northern end of our province to Flameshaven."

"And my sister and your siblings?"

"Mother is with him along with Cady and Giddy," Creetan said and then hesitated a moment before finishing, "Almas was taken again by the Lich Lords, I'm with Ulec and Lord Teanas to try to find and rescue him."

Uncle Marpel muttered something under his breath before saying out loud, "I'll help you when this battle is over. All the people brought from Jaspen have been moved back towards Forjad."

"They are coming," a voice said in his head before he could question his uncle about how the people from Jaspen had arrived there.

Sacred Knight had spoken and sure enough he could see numerous figures leaving the tree line and charging the wall.

Uncle Marpel held up his staff in front of him and put a piece of wood protruding from the staff to his lips. A deep sound resonated from his staff and Creetan realized his uncle's staff was an instrument.

A feeling of calmness and focus washed over him like it had in his first battle when Almas had used his bard skills to help him. He pulled an arrow from his quiver and notched it onto the string of his bow.

Sacred Knight spoke again, *"Channel magic through me into the arrow."*

Creetan did as he was told putting all the magic into the arrow that he could. Sacred Knight continued, *"When the command to fire comes aim for the largest group of revenants."*

The mindless undead creatures came into archer range and he heard Lord Cordwainer command the archers to release their arrows. Creetan released his and was nearly blinded as a beam of light shot out from his bow and created a cloud of undead dust in the ranks of the oncoming undead attack. Another such beam came from Lord Teanas' position with the same result. Creetan couldn't help wonder how Lord Teanas had used what he thought was a Paladin spell.

"Mimic can copy the magical abilities of any weapon it comes in contact with. Your father let Mimic touch me so that Teanas would have one more powerful weapon in his arsenal."

"Cover!" Lord Cordwainer called out at the same time Sacredknight's answered His unspoken question.

Hearing Lord Cordwainer's command, Creetan saw many of the revenants brake off bone spikes from their arms. Creetan ducked behind the parapet and heard several objects strike the wall near him and felt the stir of air as objects flew over right above his head.

"Move to another part of the wall and reload your bow. We will be a primary target for them," Creetan's fieles advised him.

"Thanks," Creetan thought back sarcastically, *"I always wanted to be a primary target."*

Creetan moved several paces down the wall keeping his head down as he prepared another arrow. He rose just long enough to unleash another blast of magical destruction on the undead before ducking back under cover. This became his pattern for what seemed to be forever; at least it was until a blast of magic blew the wall apart where he had been standing just a few moments before.

The force of the blast sent him flying forward where he

landed hard and rolled a few feet. He got into his hands and knees dazed and heard someone yelling something about the wall being breached.

Creetan looked behind him to see a portion of the wall was missing. Revenants and Kadus Knights were entering into the gap of the wall while city defenders were attempting to push them back. He saw both Lord Teanas and Ulec fighting together at the front. His uncle was also there with his staff, each swing and strike creating sounds that somehow his uncle was able to manipulate into music. Creetan could feel magic from the music still helping to give him strength and focus.

His uncle's bardic abilities did more than that however. Creetan saw him put the mouthpiece to his mouth and blow a long staticky note that seemed to fit perfectly with the music his fighting made, and when he blew that note it looked like lightning erupted from his staff the jumped from enemy to enemy, bringing down a dozen or so all around the bard.

"You don't have time to watch, you need to rejoin the fight!"

Creetan scrambled to pick up arrows that had been thrown from his quiver and scattered around him when he was struck by the blast. After stuffing as many arrows as he could into his quiver that he could quickly grab, He notched an arrow and began scanning the growing battle for a target, but the fighting was too close; the chances of hitting an ally was too great.

"Look for those in danger and use me to shield them," Sacred Knight told him.

"How?"

"Picture a shield to protect them and channel that thought and magic into me!"

Creetan saw a soldier who was in trouble and did as Sacred

Knight instructed. He extended his arm toward the struggling soldier and a golden glow surrounded him. The revenant attacking him crumbled to dust when it came in contact with the glowing shield. Creetan dropped the shield once allied soldiers came to assist him.

Suddenly there was another deafening blast down the wall as another magic explosion opened up another breach.

"How are they doing that to the wall?" Creetan wondered.

"The Kadus Knights have mages."

"Mages can do that?"

Creetan fought as he talked with Sacred Knight. Now the lich lord's forces were pouring through both breaches.

"Mages focus their magical abilities through their knowledge. Several mages combining their knowledge and magic can exploit weakness in the wall. Draw a light shield around yourself, mages are very deadly if they focus all their magic at once."

Creetan noticed a Kadus Knight approaching his Uncle Marpel who was engaged with two revenants. Calling out a warning to his Uncle, Creetan quickly sent an arrow at the knight who was able to step out of the way with barely a glance at Creetan.

He was about to send another arrow at the knight when he felt a strange sensation coming over him.

"More magic to your shield, now!" Sacred Knight warned.

Creetan poured more magic into the Holy Shield protecting him. He could feel something attacking the shield, draining it of power, draining him. Around him just outside his magic shield he could see mushrooms springing from the ground and saw the hilt of a dagger on the ground start to crumble as rust covered the metal.

"A mage is attacking you with some kind of decay spell. Keep the shield up!"

Suddenly the attack cut off. Creetan collapsed to his knees, utterly exhausted. Looking up he noticed the Kadus Knight who had been about to attack his uncle was now retreating helping a female knight who looked as wiped out as he felt. She must have been the mage. She must have put as much energy into the attack as Creetan had put into blocking it.

"Look out!" Sacred Knight warned.

Creetan saw a shadow come over him; a Kadus Knight was about to strike him with a sword. Creetan tried to put up another magic shield but knew he didn't have enough power left to stop the strike.

Suddenly a small form scooted in between him and the knight.

"Stop!" The form yelled putting both his hands up in front of him. Creetan recognized immediately who it was.

The knight angrily began to order, "Almas, Get ou–"

"Please! It's my brother," Almas pleaded.

The knight gave Creetan a strange look and asked in an unbelieving voice, "Cree?"

Creetan suddenly recognized who the knight was. It was Deleta, his older cousin that he had always followed around and idolized back when Creetan had been 3 or 4 years old. He hadn't seen him since right before Almas had been born.

The surprise soon faded from Deleta's face replaced by a colder look. Addressing Almas, he said, "You shouldn't be this far into the battle, come with me now!"

Deleta turned and started towards the rear lines of the attackers.

Almas turned to look at Creetan even as he started to follow the Kadus Knight down the stairs and off the section of wall he was still standing on.

"Almas?" Creetan said softly.

"Sorry," Almas said tears sliding down his cheeks.

Creetan dragged himself back to feet in order to follow his brother when he heard a signal horn blow.

"Fall back to the secondary wall!" Lord Cordwainer called out as he ran up to where Creetan was standing. His order was followed up by him addressing Creetan, "Please Lord Cree, come with me."

"That was my brother, I have to go after him."

"You can't help him if you're dead, we must withdraw!"

Creetan looked for his brother again but he had already disappeared in the press of men and revenants. He didn't like it, but he had no other choice.

Lord Cordwainer led him down stairs where his personal guards directed them to the rear lines where defenders were already moving past those soldiers assigned to cover the retreat. Creetan looked to the breach in the wall. He couldn't see his uncle, Ulec, or Lord Teanas anymore.

"What about Uncle Marpel?"

"He was injured and Lord Teanas took him to the rear lines already. He should be fine but right now we need to get you out of here," the lesser lord answered as he tried to hurry Creetan along.

The city's guards were now executing a slow retreat, holding the front lines of the attackers back as the defenders retreated.

Again, Lord Cordwainer urged Creetan to hurry and they

ran with the other retreating soldiers several blocks through the city to a second wall. They passed through the gate and upstairs to the wall's battlements where he found his uncle sitting

"Uncle Marpel, are you okay?" Creetan asked.

"I'm...not sure. I saw you under attack by a mage, I was moving to help you when I felt someone touch my arm. It felt like something pulled out of me...I'm not sure what. Now, when I try to play any music it's like my fingers have forgotten what to do." Uncle Marpel stuttered a bit in shock as he tried to explain.

"We will have to figure it out later. We need to get into defensive positions. Lord Vatan, just rest for a few minutes here," Lord Cordwainer instructed.

Creetan took up a position next to a large ballista that looked like it could fire two long rows of large bolts. It was positioned so that it could be pushed forward and fire down the street approaching the gate. Right now, that street was full of retreating soldiers.

The soldiers came through the gate and formed up on the training grounds that were between the walls and the keep, which was where the people of the city who hadn't already fled the city in the days before, were taking shelter.

Soon the soldiers covering the retreat came in view still engaged in their own fighting retreat. He saw that Lord Teanas was with them now.

As they began to near archer range of the wall Creetan hear Lord Cordwainer command, "Gates ready! Archers ready!"

As Creetan readied an arrow, the men on the front line suddenly in unison threw jars on the ground in front of them which erupted into large balls of fire. Jars thrown, the men turned and ran for the gate. Lord Teanas was the only exception; he slowly walked backwards with his arms outstretched as he shaped the flames into a wall holding the undead army at bay as the rest of the last of the men passed through the gate. After a moment he too turned and ran the rest of the way as the flames began to die.

Creetan joined the other archers in shooting down the first few pursuing undead to come near the walls as Teanas passed through the gates which were already closing. The ballista was pushed forward and the large bolts cut down several ranks of enemies as the gate was secured. Creetan strung another arrow as the battle continued, he was starting to recover from the effects of the mage's attack.

After sending a couple of bolts of holy magic through the ranks of the attackers, Creetan heard a voice behind him call, "You boy, firing magic from you bow. Come here!"

It was one of the soldiers who were operating the ballista. This soldier surprised him in two ways. First the soldier was about his age. Secondly, from the sound of the voice, the soldier turned out to be a girl.

The young lady and her crew were getting the ballista ready to shoot again. She looked up and motioned for him to come over again. Creetan approached her and she said, "You're down to your last few arrows; any chance you can work your magic on these?"

She indicated the bolts ready to be fired from the ballista. Creetan gave the only response he could give. "I have no idea."

"Could we?" Creetan asked Sacred Knight.

"I don't know either...I never thought to try."

Creetan spoke out loud, "I guess now is a good time to find out."

The young lady nodded. "You give it a try. When you're ready we'll push it forward and aim; then you will pull the trigger."

Creetan put one hand near the trigger and the other held onto the fieles. He pictured magic flowing from the fieles into all the bolts and pushed all the magic he had left into making it happen. All the bolts lined up and ready to fire began to glow. Creetan gave the girl a quick nod and she pushed the ballista forward with the help of her crew.

"Okay! Shoot!"

Creetan pulled the trigger and a couple dozen of beams of light shot from the ballista and through rank after rank of enemies clearing out most of the street. The remaining revenants and knights quickly retreated away from the wall and out of sight.

Cheers rang out from the top of the wall as they pulled the ballista back and began reloading.

"Well done Creetan," Uncle Marpel said stepping over to him, he seemed to be recovering quickly. "That will give us a moment to regroup while they figure out what to do about that. Are you okay?"

Creetan suddenly felt like he was about to pass out and must have looked it the way his Uncle suddenly took him by the arm to hold him up.

"I'm fine, it just took a lot out of me."

"Here, sit down here," the girl said indicating a spot he could sit up against the ballista that was out of the sun.

"Thanks," Creetan said as he sat down. His Uncle stayed

just long enough to make sure he really was okay and then left to get the defense ready for the next assault.

"Here, take a drink of water," the girl said offering Creetan a water skin. As Creetan greedily drank she continued, "Are you a paladin?"

"I'm not. My bow is Sacred Knight, a fieles made from the soul of a paladin. I'm Cree Tanis Aguerius, do you have a name?"

"Kara Bolt. So, you're Lord Forjad's grandson?"

"I am," Creetan answered before stating, "You are really good with that ballista."

"None better. I'm the best siege weapon operator in the town," Kara answered matter-of-factly.

Creetan nodded his agreement, and then after a moment he asked, "So do you know why my Uncle is here? I haven't had the chance to ask him."

"He was the one who brought the people from Jaspen," Kara answered.

"How *did* he do that?" Creetan asked.

"It was brilliant, in the basement of the keep in Jaspen they painted the wall to look like a door into the basement of the keep here in Beaver Dam. Meanwhile here they painted a doorway into the one in Jaspen. They made a magical connection between the two that created an actual doorway."

"And the people from Jaspen evacuated to here," Creetan finished.

"Then they destroyed to paintings and destroyed the spell," Kara concluded.

They sat a moment in silence before the call rose, "They're attacking again, to the wall!"

THE NECROMANCER

The alarm went down the wall and Kara and Creetan jumped back to their position. The battle was on again.

ULEC HAD FOUND A SPOT to hide between a tree trunk and a building. He had a clear view of Almas and Tornal. With so many revenants nearby, he couldn't get close enough to the lich to strike, and since he didn't know how that would affect the curse Almas was under, he didn't even know if killing Tornal would help Almas or hurt him.

Almas was being sent out to prisoners with Deleta while Tornal stayed back near an open magic gate, the coward was ready to flee to safety should any danger to his person appear.

He wasn't sure what Almas was doing to some of the prisoners but occasionally Almas would touch a prisoner which caused some kind of pain to them. Ulec could tell that whatever his best friend was doing, it horrified him.

Whatever he was doing must have been planned before the battle because there was no communication between them. In fact, Ulec had never seen Almas so quiet.

Ulec watched as his best friend went over and placed his hand on Tornal. Almas had a look of pure disgust as he did.

"He's stealing magic from them, and giving it to Tornal," came the voice from the fieles in his rusica.

Ulec had found out that his rusica was a fieles made from a piece of his mother's soul and had the same powers that his father's ring had. He had named it Changing Hand. The power to take the form of any weapon could come in very handy, but right now it didn't give him power to break the curse that held

Almas to Tornal.

"The same way he took my curse from my arm I bet," Ulec responded.

"I should've had you hold Sacred Knight before the battle started. I could have taken its form and one shot of a holy arrow could've ended him," Changing Hand lamented.

"I'm not so sure, it would be a far shot, and he has a lot of revenants in front of him. He wants to make sure no one can do to him that Lord Mason did to that other lich," Ulec observed.

The elvish boy continued to watch the Lich Lord with intense hatred for a moment longer when Changing Hand spoke again, *"Look down!"*

Ulec looked down and took a moment to recognize the small creature crawling up the tree towards him. It was one of those small undead things that Almas had used at Debigroc!

The creature stopped and looked at Ulec for a moment. Looking back up he saw Almas look right at Ulec for just a moment, just long enough to lock eyes with him. Almas then quickly looked back to the group of prisoners. As normal the undead were only keeping prisoners alive that they didn't think would be useful as revenants, meaning they were mostly children. They were moving one group through a magic gate, destined to be sacrificed before a future battle or one of Tornal's future experiments.

Ulec looked again to Almas, who gave him a brief glance again but a look full of pleading. He wanted Ulec to save the prisoners. It was clear what he was being forced to do to these people was destroying him. Ulec knew his friend wouldn't be able to stand much more of the pain he was causing. The next glance between them Ulec nodded his agreement.

THE NECROMANCER

Almas moved his hand down to his side and opened his hand and then one by one began to close his fingers into a fist. It was a countdown. Ulec let Metal out of his bag and gave him a mental command. Then he moved.

Once Almas' silent countdown reached zero, a building that was somewhat near Tornal suddenly erupted into flames. For just a few moments all the revenants that weren't searching for threats from the flaming building were putting themselves around Tornal. None, not even the prisoners, noticed that the last group of prisoners had gained one extra member, the hood of his cloak pulled tight to hide his elven ears. They also didn't notice the slime that had moved through the magic gate.

Once the undead were certain that there was no danger, they started to prepare to send the last of the prisoners through the gate when two other figures stepped out from the gate. It was an older lich and a living boy.

"Lord Lich-El," Tornal exclaimed, "You've returned."

"Tornal, how is the battle progressing?" Lich-El asked.

"Very well, we smashed through their first wall. Soon we will do the same at the wall around their keep."

"So glad to hear that, since you will be doing it without the Kadus Knights. I will be taking them to begin preparation for an attack on Flameshaven." Lich-El stated flatly.

"What? We are in the middle of a battle. How can you just take them?"

"I did not bring them into this alliance for you to use as a shield, as you have been. I will be taking personal command of them."

"What of Fireforge? Do you intend to just bypass them so we can be attacked from behind?" Tornal asked.

"Fireforge has already been emptied. Lord Gidon has evacuated the entire valley to Flameshaven

Ulec noticed Almas was staring at Lich-El with a surprised look. Something about the old lich had gotten his attention. Meanwhile the boy with Lich-El had excitedly waved to Almas when he saw him and his enthusiasm didn't seem to dip even for a moment when Almas didn't show that he even noticed the boy.

"I expect you to join us at Flameshaven as soon as you are done here," Lich-El said finishing his conversation with Tornal. He then addressed the boy that was with him, "I will be going straight to our staging ground near Flameshaven. Kade, please see these last prisoners to our main camp and put them with the rest of the prisoners. Tornal will bring them to Flameshaven when he is done here."

"What about the elf, do I take him too?" The boy casually asked as he gestured toward Ulec.

All heads turned to the group of prisoners at once. Almas looked on with a horrified expression. The boy, referred to as Kade, continued to look expectantly at Lich-El. Ulec never even saw the boy look in his direction. How had he noticed Ulec? No one ever noticed him when he didn't want to be noticed! Lich-El was the only lich that didn't seem to be surprised, he just smiled and said, "Ulec, my boy. How good to see you again. I don't believe I've seen you since you were a baby. You certainly have grown."

I took a moment for Tornal to find his words...well, word anyway. He just glared at Ulec and said, "You!"

Ulec's mind was racing. Being spotted wasn't something that ever happened to him.

Tornal looked like he was about to speak again and possibly act, as he was pulling out his staff, but Lich-El spoke first, "Yes Kade, you can take him back with the rest of the prisoners."

Tornal looked at Lich-El in astonishment. "Do you think this elvish child is just going to go quietly with him?"

Lich-El responded, "I do believe that was his intent all along."

"Of course it was! He is up to something. He probably intended to assassinate you or me!"

"No, I think he is more likely looking to rescue the prisoners. I suppose we will have to do something about that," Lich-El mused before coming to a decision, "Tornal, you will continue your attack on Beaver Dam. I will make sure Ulec is suitably restrained."

"Can I fight him?" Kade asked excitedly.

Almas was silently trying to get Kade's attention and was vigorously shaking his head. Lich-El meanwhile seemed to consider the request a moment before saying, "I suppose that would be fine, you may go ahead and be the one to restrain him."

There was something strange about this boy, he reacted to Lich-El's permission like he just got the birthday present he always wanted rather than just permitted to get in a fight that could easily end with him being killed. Ulec was still sitting among the prisoners still unsure how to get out of this. There were so many revenants around him.

"Are you seriously going to let this boy–" Tornal started to say but was cut off by Lich-El.

"Yes, I am, but this isn't your concern. Take Almas and return to your battle. Once these prisoners are secured, I will be taking the Kadus Knights as I have already said. You may leave us now."

Lich-El spoke with finality. Tornal stared in pure hate at the leader of the lich lords, and ordering Almas to follow him; he then turned and left, the magic gate vanishing as he went. Almas, looking twice as horrified as before, silently followed.

"Ulec," Lich-El called, "You may want to step away from those prisoners. We wouldn't want any of them harmed, unless you were planning on letting us restrain you without a fight."

Ulec stood up and stepped away from the prisoners. There was no way he was going to put them at risk. Kadus Knights replaced the revenants in forming a very large circle around Ulec, ensuring there was no way for him to escape. Kade stood now across from him, shaking with excitement. Ulec didn't like the idea of fighting a young boy who obviously mistook Ulec's own youthful appearance and underestimated his chances of victory.

Kade spoke, "I'm glade to meet you; Almas told me all about you. You don't have any weapons on you, do you? Here take two of my daggers."

The boy spoke in a rush and gently tossed two of his own daggers at Ulec's feet. Ulec picked up the strangely shaped daggers, he didn't want to reveal he had a fieles quite yet.

Ulec had a question of his own and asked, "How did Almas tell you so much, seeing how little talking I've seen him do?"

Kade continued speaking, now with a hint of sarcasm in his voice, as he took up a fighting position, "Tornal kept getting annoyed with him and ordered him not to speak in his glorious presence. Almas still finds ways to annoy him though. He is a genius. Are you ready to start?"

"If you think so highly of Almas, why are you trying to kill his best friend?" Ulec asked, now with Kade's daggers in either hand.

Kade shrugged, still beaming with excitement, "Just to see if I can win. How's this? If you win you can go free."

"And the prisoners?" Ulec asked.

"Sorry, I can't do anything about them, they aren't my prisoners. So, are you ready to start or what?" There was a hint of impatience in Kade's voice now.

Ulec nodded and to his surprise watched Kade throw both of his daggers to either side crossing his arms in front of him. Ulec saw the daggers arc in their flight and soon both were coming at him from either side. Ulec took a step back and the incoming daggers changed direction slightly still coming at him. So, the boy was using magic to manipulate the flight of the daggers. This fight might be harder than Ulec thought.

Ulec raised his own daggers to deflect the two spinning blades when a voice entered his head, *"Look out!"*

Ulec deflected to daggers on either side of him and at the same time jumped and kicked out to knock away the two daggers being thrust at him by Kade who had pulled out two more daggers and rushed at him while Ulec's attention was on the attacks coming from either side. This boy was very good.

In one motion Kade threw the daggers in his hands and almost simultaneously caught the other two which had arced right back to him. Ulec soon found himself fending off four daggers that relentlessly attacked him from all sides. Kade amazingly juggled the daggers, catching them as they returned and holding onto them just long enough to either strike out at Ulec or deflect one of Ulec's own attacks before throwing it in order to catch another returning dagger.

He was so focused on the fight, that Ulec almost made a fatal mistake when he stumbled in surprise when Kade started speaking to him with an almost casual tone as he fought. "Maybe later I can teach you how to throw the boomerang daggers. They are pretty awesome weapons when used right. Don't you think?"

"Duck!" Changing Hand warned

Ulec ducked and felt a breeze as a shining dagger passed right over his head.

"Careful," Kade said, "That almost had you."

Ulec said nothing, he just struck out to try to slash Kade's chest. To Ulec's astonishment something underneath deflected his blow. The boy must have had some kind of armor underneath his shirt but Ulec couldn't see any outlines of armor.

Kade smiled and said, as he tried attacking Ulec from four directions at once, "That's my Chaos Breastplate. They are very rare, only families descended from officers of the original Chaos Guard have any. When you put them on, they mold themselves right to the skin so they always fit and can't be seen. My father gave me mine."

This boy was unbelievably good for a human child. Ulec decided he needed to finish this fight. When he had an opening, he threw one of the daggers he was using at the boy.

Kade deflected the attack and saw the boy's eyebrows raise in surprise as a sword appeared in Ulec's hand swinging down at him. Before the sword could make contact, a spinning dagger struck it allowing Kade to dodge the blow.

"So, you do have a weapon of your own!" Kade exclaimed,

seemingly unfazed by his close call, "Is that a fieles?"

Again, Ulec didn't answer them. He continued to fight, only now the weapon in his right hand would change forms from time to time, but the boy was expecting it now and Ulec still couldn't seem to get through his defense. On the positive side he wasn't taking the offense any more.

Ulec was starting to get a feel for the boy's fighting technique and was starting to develop a plan when Kade switched subjects. "Hey, by the way, Almas told me about how your mother killed the lich Rynos back at Demon Mountain. How she tapped her foot and a pillar of energy came out of the ground. After talking about it with my mother—she's a scholar and a mage—I finally figured out how she cast that spell."

At the moment three of Kade's daggers were closing in on him, two from the sides and once from behind. His first attempt at an attack since Ulec revealed Changing Hand. Meanwhile Kade was in front of him. This was the fourth time that Kade had tried this four-pronged attack on him and Ulec was ready to turn it around on him. But instead of rushing forward to strike at him, Kade casually tossed the dagger so that it landed blade first into the ground. At the same time the other three daggers suddenly dropped to the ground so that he had a dagger sticking in the ground on each side of him. Ulec's fieles shouted a warning to his mind but he was only able to pull some magic around him in a poor imitation of a paladin's shield when the ground erupted beneath him. The blast wasn't nearly as powerful as the one his mother had done to Rynos but Ulec still felt himself lifted from the ground and thrown back. He landed on his back, hitting his head hard, and everything went black.

Chapter 8

"**W**ell done, Kade. You truly do have remarkable skill. How were you able to reproduce one of Lady Alixia's spells like that?"

"My mother said the ground is full of stored energy, like dead plants and bugs, oils and fats left behind by living things. All I had to do was learn all I could about them and develop a magical connection to it so I could use magic to release that energy. So, I didn't kill him like you asked. What do you want me to do with him now?"

"I will take you and the prisoners back to the main camp with a few knights to help guard the camp. You will place Ulec with the other prisoners. Make sure he is restrained and have a couple of the guards keeping an eye on him at all times."

"You know that probably won't be enough once he wakes up."

"I would suggest making it enough, unless you want to make Tornal very, very angry."

"HERE THEY COME AGAIN!"

Three times now Creetan had worked with Kara and her team to help stop the undead's relentless attacks. This 4th wave looked to be the largest so far, although he noticed there were no Kadus Knights this time.

The exhausting battle was taking its toll. Not only were they starting to run low on the darts that were fired by the ballista, but its crew was taking longer to ready it for each shot and Cree just couldn't put the magical power into the shots that he could do at the first. He just couldn't build up enough magical power between shots.

The crew of the ballista pushed the enormous crossbow forward and Creetan charged the bolts with magic and once again several beams of light shot out and ranks of revenants vanished leaving nothing but dust.

The crew pulled the crossbow back again to reload and Creetan saw a bird land on the crossbow. Thinking Ulec must be trying to tell him something, Creetan looked closer. It took a moment to realize the creature busily scratching on the ballista wasn't a bird, it wasn't even alive. It was some sort of undead creature. He was about to draw his short sword to destroy the thing when he noticed it had scratched two words on the ballista. "Cree jump!"

Remembering what had happened to the first wall, Creetan didn't hesitate. He yelled to everyone else to jump and grabbed Kara, who had stepped next to Creetan to see what he was looking at. She gave a Yelp of surprise as he pulled her with him as he jumped from the wall.

They hit the ground and rolled to help soften their impact on the ground and Creetan obeyed Sacredknight's order to shield himself with magic just in time as the wall they had just been standing on erupted in an explosion.

Once the rocks stopped falling Creetan looked up. There was a gaping hole in the wall and revenants began to pour out. Kara immediately stood up and went towards the keep. There were several small catapults lined up by the wall of the keep.

"Aim for the breach!" She ordered as she began to adjust the aim of the catapult that she took command of. In just a moment there was a series of twangs and several small barrels flew into the gap in the wall which erupted in explosive fire.

Creetan notched an arrow and looked over the battle field. The catapults had stopped the flow of undead for the moment and the guards and soldiers were handling the ones that had gotten through.

Lords Teanas and Cordwainer were in the forefront of the battle having come down from the wall which was emptying of defenders who were getting ready to make their last stand in front of the keep.

Suddenly the wall exploded in two more places on either side of the hole. Several of the catapults turned to fire upon the new breaches but something strange happened. A strange wind started blowing through the gaps in the walls.

"It's Tornal. He's using the fieles Cyclone, to control the wind." Sacred Knight said, *"Take cover!"*

The wind picked up and soon large pieces of the broken-up wall began flying through the gap. The large rocks began to smash into the catapults.

"Look out!" Creetan called as he pulled Kara away from her catapult just before it was smashed to pieces.

"I think we are in trouble," Kara declared looking at the remains of her catapult.

Revenants were now pouring out of the gaps. Creetan felt despair overcoming him. The defenders wouldn't last long against such numbers. He had failed to save Beaver Dam and he had failed to save his brother; the two main things his father had assigned him to do.

"Don't give up yet! As long as you are still breathing there is hope," Sacred Knight urged.

Creetan began firing his remaining arrows. If this was the end, then he would do as much damage as he could. He continued to fight as the defenders were slowly forced back.

After several minutes of intense fighting Sacred Knight spoke again, *"Something new is coming. Look above."*

Creetan looked up and saw two creatures flying in circles above the city. At first, he thought they were large bats but soon realized they had arms and legs. They were some sort of demons.

Kara followed Creetan's gaze and asked, "Are those imps?"

"I think they are, but what are they doing here?" Creetan answered.

As if in answer to two small demons swooped down towards the ranks of undead. As they flew over the ranks of revenants, the imps fired dozens of blasts of magic turning dozens more of the Lich Lord's army to dust.

The revenants backed off; the Lich Lords not sure what to make of the unexpected attack. Creetan and Kara moved over to where Lord Teanas was standing as one of the imps swooped down to land right in front of the elvish lord and transformed into a small elvish girl, the second imp landed and perched itself on her shoulder.

"Seacra!" Creetan exclaimed. It was Ulec's younger sister,

who like her mother could take the form of other creatures. She had gone north with her mother just before the undead had started their invasion.

Seacra didn't respond to him. She just looked at her father with fury in her eyes and asked, "Where is Ulec?"

"He was going to see if he could help Almas. I think something happened to him as he hasn't checked in with me for a while," Lord Teanas answered in a worried tone and then asked his daughter, "Where is your mother?"

"There isn't time to explain right now. Please excuse me, I have a score to settle with Tornal. Just cover me so I can end this battle and deal with him," Seacra answered with enough venom in her voice to kill the most venomous snake.

Seacra turned to face the undead and began marching towards them as the imp on her shoulder took off into the air. As she stalked away towards the Lich Lord's army she turned into the biggest and most frightening creature Creetan had ever seen. It stood at least 20 feet tall and resembled the imp except it was much, much bigger.

"That is an Elder Demon, a lord of demons," Sacred Knight said in awe.

"I thought she could only take the form of things she has touched," Creetan thought back.

"She does. Somewhere she had to have had come across an Elder Demon and survived the meeting."

The revenants reacted by attacking, but Seacra took out the first row of revenants with one swipe of her clawed hand, and began ripping through the mass of undead as the imp flew above her raining down blasts of magical energy.

"Are we sure this isn't Lady Alixia pretending to be Seacra?"

Creetan asked Lord Teanas.

"It is certainly my daughter; I will be very much interested to know what has happened up north these last several weeks." Lord Teanas responded.

"Everyone forward and attack!" Lord Cordwainer called. The rest of the defenders charged forward cutting through the revenants that Seacra missed. Soon the revenants were in full retreat. They pursued the revenants through the streets of the city.

Soon Lord Cordwainer called a halt for fear of running into an ambush. Seacra didn't halt; she turned back into an imp and flew off.

Lord Teanas motioned for Creetan to follow him and they approached Lord Cordwainer. Lord Teanas addressed him, "We will scout ahead and look for ambushes and see what is happening outside the city."

"I will go with them."

It was Uncle Marpel. He still looked pale but he had a determined look on his face. Lord Teanas nodded his agreement and the three left. They moved quickly but cautiously to the broken up outer walls.

They hid behind some rubble and looked out. They saw the undead army retreating into a magic gate. He also saw Almas with a Lich Lord holding a staff which Creetan assumed was Tornal near the gate. He saw no sign of Seacra or the imp that was with her.

"Looks like Seacra really scared them, but I still can't believe she scared them enough to make them flee like this," Creetan commented.

"It isn't just me they are running from."

THE NECROMANCER

Creetan turned around to find Seacra had appeared right by them, the imp perched on her shoulder again.

Seacra continued, "I found Lord Gidon in Flameshaven, he asked me to take a message to King Yucaipa. He and his army should be here in less than an hour. Their scouts must have spotted them."

"Seacra!" Lord Teanas addressed his daughter, "What have you and your Mother been up to since we parted?"

"I can explain better after we take care of Tornal. Short story is Mother and me were at a village of shadow hunters when we found out it was about to be attacked by and army of demons. That's where I picked up Tricker here," Seacra said indicating to the imp on her shoulder. She continued, " I ended up getting separated from Mother so I came looking for you guys. Like I said I found Lord Gidon at Flameshaven and he sent me to Yucaipa for reinforcements. Now, what more have you found out about Almas? I think I know how to help him."

They filled her in on what little they knew which wasn't much. Seacra quickly told them her plan.

When most of the undead army had gone through the magic gate, Lord Teanas approached the fleeing undead, followed by Creetan and Uncle Marpel.

"Tornal!" He called out, "We will let you leave but it is time you let Almas return to his family!"

Tornal's response was to send a group of revenants at him as he continued to evacuate his army.

Lord Teanas cut his way towards Tornal, hardly being slowed down by the small group of revenants. Watching the determined elf approaching Tornal pointed his staff at him and a whirlwind formed around Lord Teanas. However, before it could lift him off his feet and throw him, the elvish lord snapped his fingers creating a spark that quickly turned the whirlwind in to a flaming tornado, which expanded to consume the remaining revenants around Lord Teanas. For several seconds it looked to Creetan that the lich lord and the elvish lord struggled over control of the flaming whirlwind.

"Is there anything we can do?" Creetan asked.

His uncle shook his head and responded, "I can feel my abilities starting to return but not enough to help."

"You need to distract Tornal. Quickly!" Sacred Knight warned.

Creetan didn't even ask why, he just quickly notched an arrow and let it fly at Tornal. The lich lord waved his staff and the arrow changed course and flew harmlessly past, but the distraction worked and the flaming whirlwind dispersed around Lord Teanas. That was when he saw the vines of some sort of plant snaking up and around the elf's legs. They were smoking from the heat of the flaming whirlwind.

Lord Teanas started to cough and fell to his knees. He had breathed in the smoke of whatever those things were.

Tornal laughed and spoke, "Who would have thought such a weak magical ability from a farmer would be so useful."

Lord Teanas was in danger. Creetan didn't hesitate, he rushed forward to Lord Teanas and put a magic shield around them both just as Tornal shot a blast of magic at them. His shield took the blast and held and Creetan started putting as much healing magic into Lord Teanas as he could.

Tornal continued laughing, caught up in his victory over the elvish lord that he almost didn't notice that Almas had stepped close to him with a look of desperation as he watched the battle.

"Well, boy," Tornal said, "If they want you so bad...go over there and you finish them off. Take their magic and kill them.

Almas responded by grabbing Tornal's arm and Tornal sank to his knees in pain. After just a moment Tornal gave Almas a hard shove away. It was only then that he noticed a second Almas standing nearby with a surprised look on his face. It only took him a moment to figure out what was going on and opened his mouth to say something, but before he could speak, the fake Almas had turned into a fake Tornal and spoke first.

"Almas, I order you to be free and to make all your own choices from now and forever!"

Then the fake Tornal turned back into Seacra.

"Kill them all now!" Tornal bellowed.

The real Almas, still with a stunned look, faced Tornal and spoke one simple word, "No," then he smiled and said it again, "No!"

Then Almas' smile turned into a glare, and Tornal's turned into an expression of fear. Realizing the danger, he was suddenly in, Tornal leapt into his magic gate which immediately vanished. Leaving a couple dozen revenants behind.

The revenants started to withdraw but suddenly hundreds of those small undead creatures like the one Creetan had seen on the wall just appeared from bushes and other hiding places and swarmed the revenants turning them into dust in a matter of seconds. Then it was quiet.

Creetan quickly looked down to check on Lord Teanas who nodded and signaled that he would be fine, the healing magic having done its job. He then turned his attention back to his brother.

Seacra was the first to speak.

"Almas?"

She took a step forward as Creetan and the others approached.

"Stay back," Almas said the fury on his face changing to a blank, lost look.

"Almas, you're free now," Creetan said

Almas shook his head and said, "You don't understand, you don't know what they made me do. How many people are dead or hurt because of me? I was killed weeks ago; I shouldn't be here."

Creetan walked towards his little brother cautiously and spoke carefully, "You didn't hurt anyone. Tornal did. You found so many ways to save lives in spite of Tornal. That includes me, a few times I think."

Almas continued, "All those villages and towns, those were my battle plans they used!"

"And now your plans can help us stop the Lich Lords and save lives."

Creetan now stood right in front of his brother and dropped to one knee to be eye level with him. Almas' face had lost its undead features and tears were flowing freely.

Creetan put his hands on Almas' shoulders and, "Welcome back little brother," and pulled him into a hug while Almas broke down and began sobbing.

After a couple of minutes Almas suddenly pushed Creetan away.

"Lich-El is leading a huge attack against Flameshaven!

They also took Ulec! We have to go get him!"

"We will," Uncle Marpel said, "Just as soon as King Yucaipa arrives, we will figure something out. For now, we rest...and it's good to have you back.

Epilogue

Kade recognized the two Kadus Knights being brought into the hospital tent as being the two men left to guard the prisoners. He had been helping to tend those who had been too wounded to go to Flameshaven.

"What happened?" He asked.

One of the youths helping the men into the tent answered, "We found them outside the prisoners' cage, unconscious."

"Let me guess," Kade asked, "The prisoners are all gone?"

"Yes," the young man confirmed.

They got the unconscious men onto a couple of sleeping mats and Kade asked, "Did you find their tracks and see which way they went. They shouldn't have been able to get too far away."

The young man hesitated a moment and then said, "They didn't leave on foot. I think they rode away."

"Rode?" Kade asked, his eyebrows rising.

"All we found were what looked like prints from very large wolves."

"You're saying all the prisoners escaped riding on large dire wolves?" Kade asked and then said, "That...is...brilliant! Almas wasn't kidding about him, he is brilliant!"

"So, what do we do now? Almost all the grownups have

111

gone to Flameshaven."

"I don't know," Kade laughed, "but Tornal is going to be very, very angry. I think things are about to get interesting around here real soon."

He held up his hand and admired the rusica he now wore that he had taken from Ulec.

"This plan is insane; it will never work." The unspoken voice from the fieles said.

"Yes, it is. It is going to be glorious." Kade silently responded, "*Absolutely glorious.*"

Also by Marc Van Pelt:
Mathen's Flight
Fate's Foe Book 1

CHAPTER 1

MATHEN didn't go to the City of Aguares to have his life completely turned upside down. He also hadn't planned on turning the town its-self upside down. He had traveled just over a week from the City of Valen for only one thing...Rocks.

Well, stone might be a better word for it. Mathen owned more than a small number of factories that made the best stone products in all the Necromian Kingdom. He had heard of a new stone quarry outside of Aguares with unusually high quality of stone.

So, it was purely with the intent of a business deal that he found himself driving his wagon through a forest of dead trees just outside Aguares in the Yucaipan Republic. It was the 3rd such forest he and his two escorts had passed through and Mathen found himself reflecting on the changes he had seen in the world during his life. It was during the course of these reflections that a voice came to his mind.

"You should've seen this world in the day I was created. Only the most ancient elves can even imagine the life and beauty this land once enjoyed."

Mathen's hand moved to his chest and felt the shape of an ancient crest that hung from his neck under his shirt. The crest had been in his family for over 800 years but it wasn't the age that gave it its value. It was the soul locked away inside of it by ancient elvish magic. It was a fieles, which was the name given to living objects.

"*I'd rather not*", Mathen thought back. "*Just the decay in my own time is enough to make me sad. I'm not sure I can bear what could've been.*"

The Voice responded, "*You think it's hard for you? Think how some of the more ancient of the elves feel about it. In the last 800 years they have watched humans build more and more machines that aren't very friendly to nature. Just those steam engine things you guys came up with a few years ago do tend to make the air very dirty. It's no wonder they blame you guys for the decay.*"

Mathen replied, "*But we know humans aren't to blame. This decay started over a thousand years ago. All we can do is make best of the time the world has left and there is still quite a bit of time left.*"

"*Much time for you perhaps, but a blink for me. And then I'll be here long after the world dies. That's my future,*" came the response.

It was an old argument. Mathen determined to make the best of his life and the life of others while the fieles around his neck spoke of the good ol' days and complained about the present, and the future, or lack thereof.

The fieles was named Seer. Its power was to give glimpses of the future, sometimes things that would be and at times things that might be. The glimpses would come randomly, sometimes as clear visions, or at times as vague premonitions.

Despite their arguments and different opinions, the two were good friends and had developed a relationship of trust. Seer had been extremely helpful in all of Mathen's business dealings and it was on the fieles recommendation that he was now entering Aguares.

The city had spent most of the last two thousand years as a farming community. So, while it was one of the largest cities in the region it was spread out and seemed very small when compared to the cities of the neighboring kingdoms and nations.

Making the city feel smaller yet was the fact the fields had lost their fertility over the last five years. Most of the population had left and only the fates knew what the rest had done to survive since the stone quarry had opened only a few months ago.

As his wagon slowly made its way down the main street towards the center of town, he was amazed on how few people there were. There were a couple of sullen looking children sitting in front of a shop. A man dressed in rags lying on the side of the street in what appeared to be a drunken slumber. Mathen noticed his escorts kept resting their hands on the holsters of their firearms as they moved through the city.

"I've seen cities a day after being pillaged and razed with happier and more numerous people," Seer commented.

Mathen responded, *"Most left when the farms failed. Those that remain are spread out. What I wonder is how they have survived these last five years with no visible source of income."*

"Independently wealthy?" Seer asked.

"You can answer that better than me. I've been here once

before and that was 40 years ago. You've been here, what, a couple dozen times in the last 500 years?" Mathen shot back.

"Thirty-eight. And you're right. This place should've been completely abandoned within two years of the land failing. The nearby forests are all dead and rotting. The nearest source of food is a day's journey; so, all food would have to be traded for, but what do they trade with?" Seer asked.

"I've always liked a good mystery," Mathen thought as he pulled up to the hotel and looked over himself to make sure he was presentable but not overly neat.

Mathen sent his escorts in to make arrangements and stepped down from the wagon to begin tying up the horses. As he finished Seer alerted him to someone coming.

"Looks like they have a welcoming committee for you."

Turning around Mathen saw a young boy about 8 or 9 approaching him. The boy was the first smiling face he'd seen so far in town, but it was the type of smile Mathen normally associated with predators moving in of prey. On a boy that young he couldn't decide if it looked cute or disturbing.

"Welcome to Aguares, Sir!" the boy started enthusiastically. "Can I help you with your bags?"

"Thank you but I can manage myself." Mathen answered.

"You're a Necromian aren't you?"

"Yes I am. I'm from Valen, what gave me away?" Mathen asked the boy with a grin.

"Your skin is darker and the top of your ears are a little more pointy. Is it true you live a long time?" the boy asked.

The child fidgeted as he spoke, pacing a little from time to time. Mathen noticed he seemed to slowly fidget closer and closer to him.

"Yes, it's true," Mathen answered. "We have a little elvish blood in us which means we age at half the speed of full-blooded humans. I'm 108-years- old."

"What are you doing here in Aguares?"

"I'm a stone cutter. I came about the new quarry."

"Oh, you'll want to talk to Mr. Stoneman across the street," the boy replied.

Mathen looked to the building the boy pointed to which apparently was the moment the boy had waited for. After a quick warning from Seer, and without even looking, Mathen snapped his hand over to his left pocket and grabbed hold of a wrist that was already moving away. Turning around he came face to face with the boy who had both a startled look on his face and Mathen's coin bag in his hand.

It was as Mathen opened his mouth to speak that the vision struck. In all the years that Mathen had possessed Seer, he had had many visions. Hundreds in fact. But the vision he had at this moment was the longest, clearest, and most disturbing vision he had ever had. While the horrors of war, death, and unspeakable crimes he witnessed seemed to go on forever, the vision passed almost instantly in real time as all visions do.

As it ended Mathen found himself still holding the boy's wrist, the coin bag still in hand and a fearful look on his face. The boy... the boy had been the focus of the vision. He had seen glimpses of the boy's terrible future—or better said the terrible future this boy would create.

Mathen quickly tried to compose himself and managed to give the boy a smile as he plucked his coin bag from his hand.

"Thank you for finding that, I hadn't realized that I had dropped it," Mathen said.

The boy's expression changed from one of fear to one of confusion. Meanwhile Seer wasted no time in giving its own opinion.

"I don't think letting him off is a good idea. We both just saw his future, what he will become, and do. I've seen more than a few monsters in human clothing but if you let this kid go on his merry way, he'll cause more pain and suffering than any of them!"

"Whatever he may do in the future, he hasn't done yet, and right now he's still a boy. Just give me a moment to think and sort this out," Mathen thought back quickly.

Continuing to smile pleasantly at the boy, Mathen removed his coin bag and shifted his grasp to one of a simple handshake although he continued to hold the boy tight.

"It was very kind of you to pick it up for me. Let me get you something for your trouble, by the way what's your name?"

The boy's expression suddenly turned to one of suspicion.

"I thought you were here for stone."

"I am. Is there anything else I could be here for?" Mathen asked him.

The boy continued to stare at him suspiciously for a moment and seemed about to say something when they were suddenly joined by another person.

"Is there a problem here?" asked the new comer.

A man wearing a sheriff badge came over to them glancing between Mathen and the boy.

"This boy didn't try taking anything from you did he, sir?"

"I merely dropped my coin bag and the boy was good enough to retrieve it for me," Mathen responded as he released the boy's hand. The man put one hand on the child's shoulder as he studied Mathen for a few moments. He then broke out in a huge laugh and said, "Sure he did. Jas here is the most considerate boy in the orphanage. Always finding people's lost money."

He continued laughing until the boy, apparently named Jas, kicked him in the shin and took off running.

"Are you okay?" Mathen asked.

The man tried to chuckle as he rubbed the sore spot on his leg. "He's got spirit, I'll give him that. Don't worry about it; boys will be boys after all. I'm Sheriff Ajant, and you would be?"

Mathen took the hand offered him and responded, "Mathen Cutter."

Upon making contact, Mathen had hoped for another vision. There was something creepy about this Sheriff Ajant and he had hoped for something that would give him more information on what was going on. Yet he got nothing.

I don't need a vision to know there is something off about this sheriff.

Mathen ignored Seer's comment and keep his attention on the sheriff who seemed a little startled at hearing Mathen's name and was now eyeing his somewhat sloppy clothes.

"Mathen Cutter? Not the Mathen Cutter who's owner of Cutter Stoneworks?"

"The same."

Sheriff Ajant let out a long whistle, "Ain't it kind've gutsy for a man of your means to be traveling alone?"

"I've not alone," Mathen responded.

"My escorts are in the hotel making arrangements. Besides, I never travel with anything of worth. Anyone familiar with me knows that. I only carry what I need."

At that moment Mathen's escorts came out of the hotel,

"Sorry sir, but the hotel seems to be full, no rooms available."

"Full?" Mathen said with raised eyebrows glancing at the sheriff, then around the empty streets. "Is there an event in town this week?"

Sheriff Ajant got an uncomfortable and slightly suspicious look on his face and answered, "Sometimes we get an influx of travelers, other times we're empty. You happened to arrive on a full day."

"Wow, this guy must think you're as stupid as you look."

"I see," Mathen answered the sheriff, and then turned to his escorts. "See what you can find, I need to see to business here."

Mathen nodded to Sheriff Ajant politely and started across the street.

Acknowledgements

This has been a long writing process for me. The longest of any writing project. The reason being that I decided to go back to school and get my teaching license. The problem with working full time and being a full-time student is writing books gets put on hold a lot. It took a pandemic to finally give me the time to finish writing this book. So, I would first like to thank everyone who has been waiting patiently for me to finish this book and has stayed with me.

Most of all, I would like to thank my wife Tara who has supported me immensely in all my work, along with my kids who are willing to share my time with everything I do. My parents, Mike and Connie Van Pelt have also been a great source of all kinds of support as has been my Mother-In-Law Peggy Perry. Their enthusiasm helps keeps me writing.

Lastly, I would like to thank all the young people I have the privilege to associate with including nephews, nieces, and the young men and women I teach in Sunday school who also enjoy my writing and inspire me to continue. A special thanks to my nephew Spencer Perry who helped come up with the idea for one of my new characters and also to Trey Johnson who also helped to create one of my new characters and also reminded me of some loose threads from the previous books that still needed to be tied up. Thank you both for your help!

About the Author

Growing up in Bay Point, California Marc spent much of his time creating and exploring worlds and stories. He finally realized that once he got the stories written down, they stopped haunting his sleeping and waking dreams. So, he started writing them down.

He writes the kind of stories that he enjoys which are stories about families written for families.

Marc currently lives in northern Utah with his wife, and kids. He can be contacted through his Author's Facebook page at facebook.com/catseye1979

Don't miss out!

Visit the website below and you can sign up to receive emails whenever Marc Van Pelt publishes a new book. There's no charge and no obligation.

https://books2read.com/r/B-A-HGIT-SWWZB

BOOKS 2 READ

Connecting independent readers to independent writers.

Also by Marc Van Pelt

Fate's Foe
Mathen's Flight

The Lich Lord Wars
Lich-El
Escape Through the Sacred Forest
The Necromancer

Standalone
Stories From the World of Mundial

Watch for more at Facebook.com/catseye1979.

Lightning Source UK Ltd.
Milton Keynes UK
UKHW020958180123
415553UK00014B/949

9 798201 767013